LONDON

BOULEVARD

LONDON
BOULEVARD

KEN BRUEN

MINOTAUR BOOKS ❧ NEW YORK

LONDON BOULEVARD. Copyright © 2001 by Ken Bruen. All rights reserved.
Printed in the United States of America. For information, address St. Martin's
Press, 175 Fifth Avenue, New York, N.Y. 10010.

www.minotaurbooks.com

The Library of Congress has cataloged the hardcover edition as follows:

Bruen, Ken.
    London Boulevard / Ken Bruen.—1st U.S. ed.
       p. cm.
    ISBN 978-0-312-56168-0
    1. Ex-convicts—England—Fiction. 2. Criminals—England—Fiction.
3. London (England)—Fiction. I. Title.
    PR6052.R785L66 2009
    823'.914—dc22
                                                                    2009012745

ISBN 978-0-312-65042-1 (trade paperback)

Originally published in Great Britain by the Do-Not Press

First Minotaur Books Paperback Edition: November 2011

10 9 8 7 6 5 4 3 2 1

This book is dedicated to:

      USA

           Bernadette Kennedy

      Ireland

           Dr. Enda O'Byrne

PART ONE

SHOWTIME

LEARNT THIS in prison. Compulsive is when you do something repetitively. Obsessive is when you think about something repetitively.

'Course, I learnt some other stuff too. Not as clear-cut. Not as defined.

The day of my release, the warden had me up for a talk.

Bent over his desk, he kept me waiting. His head over papers, a model of industry. He had a bald patch, like Prince Charles. That made me feel good. I concentrated on it. Finally, he looks up, says,

"Mitchell?"

"Yes, sir?"

I could play the game. I was but a cigarette away from freedom. I wasn't going to get reckless. His accent was from up north somewhere. Polished now but still leaking Yorkshire pudding and all that decent shit. Asked,

"You've been with us now for?"

Like he didn't know. I said,

"Three years, sir."

He hmmphed as if he didn't quite believe me. Riffled through my papers, said,

"You turned down early parole."

"I wanted to pay me debt in full, sir."

The screw standing behind me gave a snort. For the first time, the warden looked directly at me. Locked eyes. Then,

"Are you familiar with recidivism?"

"Sir?"

"Repeat offenders, it's like they're obsessed with jail."

I gave a tiny smile, said,

"I think you're confusing obsession with compulsion," and then I explained the difference.

He stamped my papers, said,

"You'll be back."

I was going to say,

"Only in the repeats,"

but felt Arnie in *The Terminator* would be lost on him. At the gate, the screw said,

"Not a bright idea to give him lip."

I held up my right hand, said,

"What else did I have to offer?"

Missed my ride.

What the Yanks say. I stood outside the prison, waiting on my lift. I didn't look back. If that's superstition, then so be it. As I stood on the Caledonian Road, I wondered if I looked like a con, ex-con.

Shifty.

Yeah, and furtive. That too.

I was forty-five years old. Near 5' 11' in height, weighed in at 180 pounds. In shape, though. I'd hammered in at the gym and could bench press my share. Broken through the barrier to free up those endorphins. Natural high. Shit, do you ever need that inside. Sweat till you peak and beyond. My hair was white but still plentiful. I had dark eyes, and not just on the outside. A badly broken nose near redeemed by a generous mouth.

Generous!

I love that description. A woman told me so in my twenties. I'd lost her but hung on to the adjective. Salvage what you can.

A van pulled up, sounded the horn. The door opened, and Norton got out. We stood for a moment. Is he my friend?

I dunno, but he was there. He showed up, friend enough. I said,

"Hey."

He grinned, walked over, gave me a hug. Just two guys hugging outside Her Majesty's jail. I hoped the warden was watching.

Norton is Irish and unreadable. Aren't they all? Behind all the talk is a whole other agenda. He had red hair, pasty complexion, the build of a sly greyhound. He said,

"Jaysus, Mitch, how are you?"

"Out."

He took that on board, then slapped my arm, said, "Out . . . that's a good one. I like that . . . Let's go. Prison makes me nervous."

We got in the van, and he handed me a bottle of Black Bush. It had a green bow. I said,

"Thanks, Billy."

He looked almost shy, said, "Aw, it's nuttin' . . . for your release . . . the big celebration is tonight . . . and here . . ." He produced a pack of Dunhills. The lush red luxury blend. Said,

"I thought you'd be gasping for a tailor made."

I had the brown paper parcel they give you on release. As Norton started the engine, I said,

"Hold on a sec." And I slung the parcel.

"What was that?"

"My past." I opened the Bush, took a long, holy swallow. It burned. Wow, did it ever. Offered the bottle to him. He shook his head.

"Naw, not when I'm driving."

Which was rich, him being half in the bag already. He was always this side of special brews. As we headed south he was rabbiting on about the party. I switched off.

Truth is, I was tired of him already.

Norton said, "I'll give you the scenic tour."

"Whatever."

I could feel the whiskey kicking in. It does all sorts of weird shit to me, but mainly it makes me unpredictable. Even I can't forecast how it will break.

We were turning from Marble Arch and, of course, got caught at the lights. A guy appeared at the windshield and began to wipe it with a dirty cloth. Norton yelled,

"These fuckin' squeegees, they're everywhere!"

This guy didn't even make an effort. Two fast wipes that left skid marks on the glass. Then he appeared at my window, said,

"Four quid, matey."

I laughed, rolled the window down, and said,

"You need another line of work, pal."

He had long, greasy hair down to his shoulders. His face was thin, and he had the eyes I'd seen a hundred times on the yards. The eyes of the bottom-rung predator. He leant his head back and spat. Norton went,

"Aw Jaysus."

I didn't move, asked,

"You got a tire iron?"

Norton shook his head,

"Mitch, Jesus, no."

I said, "OK."

And got out.

The guy was surprised but didn't back off. I grabbed his arm and broke it over my knee. Got back in the van, and the lights changed. Norton revved fast, crying,

"Oh God, Mitch, you crazy bastard. You're out . . . what? Ten minutes . . . and you're at it already. You can't be losing it."

"I didn't lose it, Billy."

"What, you smash the guy's arm, that's not losing it?"

"If I'd lost it, I'd have broken his neck."

Norton gave me an anxious look, said,

"You're kidding . . . right?"

"What do you think?"

NORTON SAID, "I think you'll be surprised at the place I found for you."

"As long as it's near Brixton."

"It's Clapham Common. Since you've been . . . away . . . it's become trendy."

"Oh shit."

"Naw, it's OK . . . Anyway, a writer guy got into heavy schtook to some moneylenders, had to do a runner. Left everything: clothes, books . . . you're set."

"Is Joe still at the Oval?"

"Who?"

"*Big Issue* seller."

"I don't know him."

We were coming up to the Oval. I said,

"He's there. Pull over."

"Mitch . . . you want to buy the *Big Issue* now?"

I got out, walked over. Joe hadn't changed. He was disheveled, dirty, cheerful.

I said, "Hi, Joe."

"Mitchell . . . Good Lord, I heard you was doing a stretch."

I handed over a fiver, said,

"Give us a copy."

We didn't mention the change. He asked,

"Did they hurt you in there, Mitch?"

"Not so's you'd notice."

"Good man. Got a smoke?"

I gave him the pack of Dunhills. He examined them, said,

"Flash."

"Only the best for you, Joe."

"You'll have missed the World Cup."

And a whole lot more besides. I asked,

"How was it?"

"We didn't win it."

"Oh."

"There's always the cricket."

"Yeah, there's always that."

THREE YEARS in prison, you lose
  time
  compassion
  and the ability to be surprised.

I WAS nigh amazed when I saw the apartment. The whole ground floor of a two-story house. And it was beautifully furnished, all soft pastels and wall-to-wall books. Norton stood behind to gauge my reaction.

I said, "Christ."

"Yeah, isn't it something? Come and see more."

He led me into the bedroom. Brass double bed. He threw open the wardrobes, packed full with clothes. Like a salesclerk, Norton said,

"You've got your

Gucci

Armani

Calvin Klein

and other bastards I can't pronounce. Get this, the sizes are medium to large."

"I can do medium."

Back into the living room, Norton opened a drinks cabinet. Full too. Asked,

"Whatcha fancy?"

"A beer."

He opened two bottles, handed me one. I asked,

"No glass?"

"No one drinks outta glasses anymore."

"Oh."

"*Sláinte*, Mitch, and welcome home."

We drank. The beer tasted great. I indicated the place with my bottle, asked,

"Just what kind of a hurry was the guy in to leave all this?"

"A big hurry."

"Won't the loan shark want some of it?"

Norton smiled, said, "I've already had the choice bits."

It took me a minute. Blame the beer. I said,

"You're the moneylender?" Big smile. He was proud, been waiting, said,

"Part of a firm—and we'd like you on board."

"I don't think so, Billy."

He was expansive.

"Hey, I didn't mean right away. Take some time, chill out."

Chill out.

I let it go, said,

"I dunno how to thank you, Billy. It's incredible."

"No worries. We're mates . . . right?"

"Right."

"OK, I gotta go. The party's in the Greyhound at eight. Don't be late."

"I'll be there. Thanks again."

BRIONY'S A BASKET case. A true, out-and-out nutter. I've known some seriously disturbed women. Shit, I've dated them, but up against Bri they were models of sanity. Bri's husband died five years ago. Not a huge tragedy, as the guy was an asshole. The tragedy is that she doesn't believe he's gone. She keeps seeing him on the street and, worse, chats to him on the phone. Like the genuine crazies, she has moments of lucidity. Times when she appears

rational

coherent

functional

. . . then wallop. She'll blindside you with an act of breathtaking insanity.

Add to this, she has a beguiling charm, sucks you in. She looks like Judy Davis, and especially how Judy Davis appeared with Liam Neeson in the Woody Allen movie. Her hobby is shoplifting. I dunno why she's never been caught, as she does it with a recklessness beyond belief. Bri is my sister. I rang her. She answered on the first ring, asked,

"Frank?"

I sighed. Frank was her husband. I said,

"It's Mitchell."

"Mitch . . . oh Mitch . . . you're out."

"Just today."

"Oh, I'm so happy. I've so much to tell you. Can I make you dinner? Are you hungry? Did they starve you?"

I wanted to laugh or cry.

"No . . . no, I'm fine . . . listen, maybe we could meet tomorrow."

Silence.

"Bri . . . are you still there?"

"You don't want to see me on your first night? Do you hate me?"

Against all my better judgment, I told her about the party. She instantly brightened, said,

"I'll bring Frank."

I wanted to shout, "Yah crazy bitch, get a grip!" I said, "OK."

"Oh Mitch, I'm so excited. I'll bring you a present."

Oh God.

"Whatever."

"Mitch . . . can I ask you something?"

"Ahm . . . sure."

"Did they gang rape you? Did they?"

"Bri, I gotta go, I'll see you later."

"Bye, baby."

I put the phone down. Wow, I felt drained.

* * *

I HAD a sort through the wardrobe. When you've worn denim and a striped shirt for three years, it was like Aladdin's Cave.

First off I got a stack of Tommy Hilfiger out. Put that in a trash bag. All that baggy shit, maybe Oxfam could off-load it. There was a Gucci leather jacket, nicely beat up. I'd be having that. Lots of Hennes white T-shirts: the type Brando immortalized in *On the Waterfront.* The guys in prison would kill for muscular American T-shirts.

No jeans.

No problem.

Gap khaki pants, a half dozen. A blazer from French Connection and sweatshirts from Benetton.

I dunno if that guy had taste, but he sure had money. Well, loan-shark money.

There was a Barbour jacket and a raincoat from London Fog. No shit, but I'd be a con for all seasons. Odd thing was, not a shoe in sight. But was I complaining? Was I fuck. I had a pair of shoes.

Took a hot shower and used three towels to dry off. They'd been swiped from the Holiday Inn so were soft and friendly. What I most wanted was another beer, but I knew I'd better cool it. The evening ahead would be liquid and perhaps lethal. I needed to at least arrive soberish. Took a quick scan of the books, one whole wall devoted to crime writers. Spotted

Elmore Leonard

James Sallis

Charles Willeford

John Harvey

Jim Thompson

Andrew Vachss.

And that was only the first sweep. Phew! I might never go out. Just bury myself in crime.

I put on a T-shirt, khaki pants and the leather jacket. Checked it out in the mirror. No doubt I could pass for a Phil Collins roadie. Thought—"If I'd money, I'd be downright dangerous."

WALKING DOWN CLAPHAM COMMON, a woman smiled at me. I knew it was the jacket. There's a transport café in Old Town that used to be the business. It was still there. The type of place if it's not on the table, it's not on the menu.

For an ex-con there can be few greater pleasures than to eat alone. Grabbing a booth I luxuriated in just having it to myself. Knew exactly what I'd order.

The carbohydrate nightmare, neon-lit in medical overload. Like this:

Two Sausages

Mess of Bacon

Fried Tomatoes

Eggs

Black Pudding

Toast

Pot of Stewed Tea

Oh yeah.

In the booth next to me was an old codger. Eyeing me. He

had the face and manner of a "character." His name would be Alfred.

'Course, everyone would love him. Alfred would have his own corner in the pub and his own pewter tankard.

He'd be a holy terror to a new barman.

My food arrived, and he said,

"That food, son . . . you know where it comes from?"

Without lifting my head, I said,

"I've a feeling you're going to enlighten me."

That startled him, but not enough to stop him. He said,

"Big fellah like you, you should have a feed of potatoes."

I raised my head, looked at him, said,

"Old fellah like you, you should mind your own business."

Shut him down.

I tried not to wolf the food. Now that I was out, I was going to have to readapt. When I finished, I went and paid. On my way out, I stopped by Alfred, said,

"Nice chatting with you."

Walked down to Streatham and into the bank. I wasn't sure how much money I had, as they don't send statements to prison.

What they should do is send bankers there.

I filled out a withdrawal slip and got in line. It was slow, but I knew how to kill time.

The cashier was friendly in that vacant money way. I handed her the slip; she ran it by the computer, said,

"Oh."

I said nothing. She said,

"This is a dormant account."

"Not anymore."

She gave me the look. The leather jacket wasn't cutting any ice. She said,

"I'll have to check."

"You do that."

A man behind me sighed, asked,

"Is this going to take long?"

Gave him a bank smile, answered,

"I've absolutely no idea."

The cashier returned with a suit. He was Mr. Efficiency, said,

"Mr. Mitchell, if you could step over to my desk."

I could. I sat and looked at his desk. A sign proclaimed

WE REALLY CARE

He did bank stuff for a bit, then,

"Mr. Mitchell, your account has been dormant for three years."

"Is that against the law?"

Ruffled him.

Recovered,

"Oh no . . . it's ahm . . . let's see . . . with interest you have twelve hundred pounds."

I waited. He asked,

"I take it you wish to reactivate the account?"

"No."

"Mr. Mitchell, might I suggest a prudent reserve? We have some very attractive offers for the small saver."

"Give me my money."

"Ahm . . . of course . . . you wish to terminate your account?"

"Leave a pound in it . . . 'cos you guys care so much."

I got my cash but no warm handshake or cheerful good-bye.

You have to ask yourself how much it is they *really* care.

PARTY TIME. I'd had a nap and woke with a start. My heart was pounding and sweat cascading down my back. Not because I thought I was still in prison but because I knew I was out. The guys in the joint had cautioned me,

"Nothing's scarier than being out there."

Which I guess is why so many go back.

Aloud I vowed—"The fuck I'm going back."

DID A hundred sits, a hundred presses, and felt the panic ebb.

The kitchen was stocked with provisions.

No porridge, thank Christ. Had some OJ and bad burnt toast. There was a microwave, and I zapped some coffee. It tasted like shit, which was exactly what I was accustomed to. Did the shower stuff and skipped shaving. Let that three-day beard kick in.

What's the worst that could happen?

I'd look like George Michael's father.

Slapped on a Calvin Klein deodorant. It said on the label, NO ALCOHOL. Gee, no point in having a slug, then.

Sat for a moment and rolled a smoke. Had the craft down. Could do it with one hand. Now, if I could strike a match off my teeth I'd be a total success.

Took a cruise through the music collection. Oddly, for such a state-of-the-art place, the guy hadn't joined the CD revolution. It was your actual albums or cassettes. OK by me.

Put on Trisha Yearwood. A track called "Love Wouldn't Lie to Me."

Listened twice.

I'm from southeast London. We don't use words like "beauty" unless it's cars or soccer. Even then, you better know your company real good.

This song was beautiful. It stirred in me such feeling of

yearning

loss

regret.

Shit, next I'd be missing women I'd never met. Maybe it's a "being in your midforties" thing.

I shook myself, time to rock 'n' roll. Put on the Gap khaki pants—very tight in the waist, but hey, if I didn't breathe, I'd be fine. A white T-shirt and the blazer.

Looking sharp.

Like a magnet for every trainee mugger.

The album was still running, and Trisha was doing a magic duet with Garth Brooks.

Had to turn it off.

No two ways, music will fuck your head nine ways to Sunday.

WHAT YOU REGARD AS A SMALL, isolated incident sets off a chain of events you could never have anticipated. You believe you're making choices and all you're doing is slotting in the pieces of a foreordained conclusion.

Deep, huh!

I took the subway to the Oval. The Northern Line was at its usual irritating best. Two bedraggled buskers were massacring "The Streets of London." I gave them a contribution in the hope they might stop.

They didn't.

As soon as they finished, they began it anew. Coming out at the Oval, Joe was there with the *Big Issue.* I said,

"Wanna go to a party, Joe?"

"This *is* my party, Mitch." Argue that.

Across the road an Aston Martin pulled in at St. Mark's Cathedral. A young woman got out. From the trees at the church, two predators materialized. These are not the homeless, they're what Andrew Vachss calls "skels": bottom feeders. They began to hassle her. I debated getting involved. I didn't want to spoil the blazer. Joe said,

"Go on, Mitch."

I crossed the road. They'd the urban ambush going.

One in front doing the verbals, the other behind about to strike.

I shouted,

"Yo, guys."

All three turned. These preds were early twenties, white and nasty.

The first said,

"Whatcha want, jerk-off?"

The other,

"Yeah, fuck off, asshole."

Close up I saw one pred was a woman. I said,

"Leave the lady be."

The first pred read the blazer, read me wrong, moved up, said,

"Whatcha gonna do about it, cunt?"

I said,

"This."

And jammed my index finger in his right eye. It's a common maneuver in the yard. When it's serious you pop the eyeball.

This wasn't. It hurts like a bastard, though. I moved to the second pred, said,

"I'm going to break your nose."

She ran.

The woman, the would-be victim, just stared at me. I said,

"Not a smart place to park."

I recrossed the road and could hear music from the Greyhound.

Prayed it wasn't "The Streets of London."

The pub was packed. A banner over the bar proclaimed,

WELCOME HOME MITCH

Norton, in an Armani suit, greeted me warmly, said,

"Here's a Revolver."

"What?"

"It's a cocktail."

"What's in it?"

"What else but Black Bush, two jiggers of Cointreau and ginger ale?"

"Thanks, Billy, but I'll have a pint o' bitter."

Various Grade B villains approached and shook my hand. The A List were seated and expected me to approach them.

I did.

The party was what Dominick Dunne calls "a rat fuck." Too many people. Promises of sundry jobs were made and lotsa "call me" expressions. I spotted Tommy Logan, an up-and-coming drug lord, asked,

"Tommy, can I have a word?"

"Sure, son."

He was half my age. He said,

"You're looking fit."

"But for what, eh?"

We laughed politely at this. I asked,

"I need a favor, Tommy."

He moved me to the end of the bar. Out of earshot if not out of reach. I took a deep breath, said,

"I need some gear."

It was Tommy's business not to show what he felt or thought. He registered near amazement, said,

"I never had you down for the needle."

"It's a one-off, for a friend."

"Jeez, Mitch, that's the hook . . . just once."

Next he'd be giving me a lecture. I cut to the chase, asked,

"Can you do it? I'd need the works too. A hypo . . . like that."

"Sure, I'll have it for you by close of business."

He shook his head, then,

"I like you, Mitch, so all I'm gonna say is take it easy."

"Iris DeMent has a song called 'Easy.'"

"Who?"

B RIONY ARRIVED LOOKING like a radiant bag lady. She was dressed in some kind of designer trash bag. She gave me a huge hug, asked,

"Do you like my dress?"

"Ahm . . ."

"I stole it from Vivienne Westwood's shop."

Before I could reply, she asked,

"Mitch, would you like a Glock?"

"I've already turned down a Revolver."

She looked disappointed, said,

"It's a 9 mm."

"Jesus, Bri, you're serious."

She reached in her handbag, saying,

"I'll show you."

I grabbed her hand, pleaded,

"Christsake, don't pull a gun in this crowd . . . I'll get it later, OK?"

"OK, Mitch."

Norton shouted,

"Bri, whatcha drinking?"

"Harvey Wallbanger."

A woman came into the pub. It was the Aston Martin lady. I said to Bri,

"Excuse me."

"Frank will be here later, Mitch."

The late Frank. I approached the woman, said,

"Hello again." She nearly jumped, then got composure, said,

"I never got to thank you."

"Glad to help . . . did you follow me in here?"

"What? Good Lord, no . . . I'm here on a story."

My heart sank.

"You're a journalist?"

"Yes, any gathering of southeast villains is news."

She looked toward the bar. A group of grim men were deep in conversation. They exuded menace. She said,

"That looks like a nasty bunch."

"You're right. They're the police."

She laughed, asked,

"Are you serious?"

"Would you like a drink?"

"Some mineral water . . . I'm Sarah."

"Mitch."

I considered spiking the mineral water, loosen her up a bit. Then decided to just let it play. As she took a sip, she said,

"I believe the party's for a villain who's just out of prison."

"That's me."

"Oh."

I drank some beer, said,

"I'm not a criminal. I'm simply unemployed."

She digested this, then,

"What type of work do you do besides rescuing women?"

"You name it, I can do it."

"Handyman, are you?"

She considered, then asked,

"I'd have to check, do you you have a phone?"

I gave her the number and asked,

"Aren't you wary of recommending an ex-con?"

"If you get the job, it's you who'd need to be careful."

I laughed, not taking her seriously.

The first in a line of very bad judgments.

SARAH MOVED away, to do research I guess. Later, Tommy Logan approached, slipped me a package. I said,

"I owe you one, Tommy."

Bri grabbed me, said,

"Mitch, I've just met a divine young man."

"Uh-huh."

She was holding the hand of a punk. Nineteen or twenty years old. He looked like a sick David Beckham, but he had the essential smirk of the wannabe gangster. He said,

"Yo, bro."

Unless you're black, there is truly no answer to this. Except a slap up the side of the head, but I wasn't in the mood. Bri gushed,

"Mitch. I told him you'll take him under your wing."

"I don't think so."

She seemed genuinely surprised.

"You don't like him?"

"Bri, I don't know him and I don't want to know him, now give it a rest."

She disappeared into the crowd. I mingled for a while more, then figured I'd enough. Saw Norton and said,

"Billy, I'm gonna split."

"What . . . already?"

"I'm used to early nights."

"Oh right . . . listen, about the job . . ."

"The moneylending?"

"It's not like you think. You'd only need to come with me once or twice a week."

"Billy . . ."

"No, listen . . . the pad you're in, the clothes—I don't need to tell you there's no free lunches."

So much for any feeble principles. I wanted the apartment, the clothes, the life. I asked,

"When?"

"Is Wednesday good? I'll collect you 'round noon."

"Noon?"

"Yeah, our clients aren't early risers. That's why the dumb fucks are always broke."

AS JACK Nicholson said in *Terms of Endearment*,

"I was just inches from a clean getaway."

I'd got to the door when Tommy Logan called me, said, "There's a ruckus out back."

"Like I give a shit."

"You should. It's your sister."

I briefly thought of leaving her to it, then spat,

"Fuck."

Headed back there. Past stacked beer crates, empty barrels, into the yard. The punk was against the wall, a deep gash down his cheek. Bri had the Glock in his face. I said,

"Bri . . . Bri, it's Mitch."

She didn't move, said,

"He wanted to put his thing in my mouth."

I moved closer, said,

"I thought the gun was my present."

"It is."

"Well, let's have it, then, eh?"

She stared hard at the punk, then said,

"OK," and handed it to me.

He appeared on the verge of passing out. Sank down to a sitting position, blood streaming from the gash. I bent to him, began to go through his pockets. Bri asked,

"You're robbing him?"

Not that she cared, she was just curious. I said,

"I'm looking for his stash; he's a cokehead, I saw his sniffles earlier."

"You're going to do a line?"

I found the packet, ripped it open. I spread the coke along the gash, and it stemmed the blood.

Bri asked,

"What are you doing?"

"It's an anesthetic."

"How do you know?"

"I celled with a doper."

I stood up, took her arm, said,

"Let's go."

When I got her outside, she asked,

"Wanna go clubbing?"

I hailed a cab, got her in it, said,

"I'll call you tomorrow."

"Mitch, I hope you don't mind that Frank didn't make it."

"No no, I don't mind."

Heading for the subway, I had heroin, a gun and half a bag of coke. Jesus, what more could you ask of a night on London town?

BACK AT the apartment, I kicked off my shoes, opened a beer and collapsed on the sofa. Sat up after a bit and laid down a line of coke, snorted it fast. In no time, I was numb.

Fucking A.

I'd told Bri the truth about celling with a doper. He'd told me about smack, about kissing God. To hit the very stars.

I'd resolved to try it one time on my first night of freedom.

Night after night, he'd relive his first spike. As if all your life you're living in darkness and suddenly you step into the light. You laugh out loud. Your nerves feel like velvet, and your skin glows. And the energy, like you're fucking bionic.

Too, he told me about the downside. I figured I could hack it.

But not tonight. It didn't feel right. I went into the bedroom and stashed the gear under the sweatshirts. I put the Glock under my mattress. With the coke, I was up, pacing. Went to the bookshelf and picked out James Sallis.

Poetry.

Loss.

Addiction.

Perfect.

ABOUT HALFWAY through my stretch, I got a visit from the chaplain. I was lying on my bunk, reading. My cellmate was at an AA meeting. The chaplain had manners, asked,

"Might I come in?"

"Sure."

Any diversion. He sat on the opposite bunk, scanned my line of books. There was

philosophy

literature

thrillers

poetry.

He said, "Your reading is eclectic."

I thought he said electric, answered,

"Whatever gets you wired."

He gave a religious smile, all front, no warmth, said, "No—*eclectic*, it means random."

I liked it, said,

"I like it."

He picked up a volume of poetry, said,

"Rilke, now that's surprising."

I tried to remember the line, tried,

"Everything terrible is something that needs our love." It worked. He was stunned. I pushed, asked,

"The cons here, do you think they need love?"

He went evangelical, said,

"Most of the men here aren't terrible, just . . ."

But he couldn't find an appropriate adjective. I said, "You obviously haven't chowed down with us. Yesterday a guy got knifed in the face for his crème caramel."

"How unfortunate."

"That's one way of putting it."

I sat up, rolled a cig, offered the chaplain.

"No, but thank you."

I was half interested in him, asked,

"Do you drive?"

"Excuse me?"

"A car. I just like to hear about motors."

"No, I ride a bike."

Of course.

He folded his hands on his knees, adapted his face to empathy mode, asked,

"Is anything troubling you?"

I laughed out loud, indicated the world outside the cell, answered,

"Take a wild guess."

"It's good to share."

"Keep your voice down, Padre. That talk could spark a riot."

He stood up, his duty done, said,

"You're an interesting man. Might I visit on another day?"
I lay back on the bunk, said,
"My door is always open."
'Course, he never did visit again.

NEXT MORNING I was listening to the Capitol station when the phone went. Picked it up, said,

"Yeah."

"Mitch? This is Sarah."

"Right. Did you get a story?"

"No, but I might have got you a job."

"Thanks."

"Don't thank me yet. I have an aunt in Holland Park. She lives in a huge house, and it's in dire need of repairs. The snag is she's a difficult woman and no other workmen will go there anymore. Believe me, she's had an army of them."

"Why will I be different?"

Long pause, then,

"Well, she'll forgive a man anything if he's handsome."

"Oh."

"Do you want to give it a whirl? She'll pay awfully well."

"Sure, why not."

"She lives at the Elms; you can't miss it, just after the beginning of Holland Park, it has an impressive driveway."

"I'll find it."

"I'm sure you will. Do you know anything about the theater?"

"Not a thing."

"You won't have come across Lillian Palmer, then."

"Never heard of her."

"I don't suppose it matters. Anyway, that's her, my aunt."

"I look forward to meeting her."

"Don't be so sure. Well, good luck."

I decided to chance it, felt I might be on a roll, asked, "Listen, Sarah, do you fancy a drink sometime?"

"I don't think so. I'm not part of the package."

And she hung up.

So much for the roll.

I had no equipment for work but figured I'd make it up as I went along. I know enough cowboys to borrow almost anything.

First off, I'd go and see the place, see what I'd need. If I was to be a handyman, I thought casual clothes would be best. Sweatshirt and jeans should be fine.

As I headed for the subway, I thought, "I've a home, clothes, job offers, and I've only been out twenty-four hours."

Those cons had got it wrong; life on the outside was a breeze.

IN ALCOHOLICS Anonymous, they refer to HP. It means higher power. On the street they also refer to HP . . . for homeless person. The connection between both is booze. Alcoholics have to abstain to survive. The homeless depend on it to survive.

I dunno what set this off in my head. A legacy of jail is this traveling on a tangent of thought.

Whatever, by the time I snapped out of it, I was nearing Holland Park. I got off the train at Notting Hill and walked up. Found the Elms, no problem. Like Sarah said, there was a huge driveway. Strolled up, looking at the trees that lined the way.

Then the house and I muttered—"Wow."

It was a mansion, no other description would apply.

It shouted,

WEALTH.

I moved to the door, made of solid oak. Up close the house looked run-down, shabby even. Lots of work here. I lifted the heavy knocker, gave it a wallop.

The door opened. A butler stood there in full regalia. I couldn't believe it. I thought all the butlers had gone to California or sitcoms or both. He was small and sturdy. In truth, like Oddjob from the Bond movie. I was too taken aback to speak. He asked,

"Yes?"

I gave my name, mentioned Sarah and expected the bum's rush.

He said, "Madam is expecting you. Come this way."

I did.

Into a large hall. He'd have taken my coat if I had one. Led me to a drawing room and said,

"Madam will appear presently."

Then he fucked off.

The room was vast, with Regency furniture. I know that 'cos it looked like no one ever sat on it. Hundreds of framed photographs with a blond woman in them all. She looked like a laid-back Lauren Bacall with the ferocity. A massive portrait above the fireplace. The blonde again. On the walls were framed posters with LILLIAN PALMER IN STREETCAR, SWEET BIRD OF YOUTH, DESIRE UNDER THE ELMS

Like that.

Despite the expensive frames they looked old. Heavy drapes covered the windows, and I figured I'd let a little light in.

Pulled them back to reveal bay windows. An overgrown garden stretched all the way back. Without thinking, I began to roll a cig. Lit up. I was staring out the window when a shout nearly put me through it.

"PUT OUT THAT CIGARETTE!"

I turned round to face whoever. A woman brushed past me, screaming,

"How dare you open those drapes? The light will ruin the posters!"

As she covered the windows I got a look. She was dressed in a long black gown. Blond hair down her back. Then she turned.

Not at all like Bacall. More like John Cassavettes's wife, who I'd seen in *Gloria*.

I'm bad at ages but I reckoned she was an expensive sixty.

Money and care had helped keep the face intact. She had startling blue eyes and used them to scrutinize me, then,

"I presume you're here for an interview. Well? Speak up. What have you to say?"

Her voice was deep, almost coarse. The timbre that cigarettes
and whiskey add. 'Course, arrogance helps too. I said,

"I need an ashtray."

She indicated a large crystal dish. I stubbed out the cig.

It's hard to credit, but the butt threw the room off. In that
dish, the lone stub seemed like an affront. I wanted to put it in
my pocket. She said,

"You expect to make a good impression by dressing like a
runner?"

I said, "You don't have to be nice to me. I want the job."

She stepped forward, and I thought she was going to hit me,
then she laughed. A deep down and dirty one. The best kind.

Then she said,

"Sarah mentioned you'd been in jail. What are you, a thief?"

With more edge than I intended, I said,

"I'm not a thief."

"Oh dear, have I hit a nerve? Have I violated some convict
code of ethics?"

This was delivered in a dramatic voice. As if she was onstage.
I'd learn that she was never off it. I said,

"I was in a fight, it got out of hand."

Closing the topic, she said,

"There'll be no fighting here."

From out of left field, I felt a flash of desire. I couldn't believe
it. My body was responding to her. She gave a knowing smile,
and I didn't want to analyze that. No way. She said,

"We'll give you a week's trial. Jordan will set your duties."

She went to the door, stopped, said,

"If you absolutely must steal an item, take that disgusting ashtray."

And she was gone.

I FOLLOWED Jordan outside to the garage. More like an airplane hangar. The first thing I noticed was a car, up on blocks. I gave a low whistle, asked,

"Is that what I think it is?"

"Yes, it is."

I tried to place his accent, ventured,

"Are you German?"

"Hungarian."

He swept his arm round the garage, said,

"Everything you could possibly need is here."

Tools.

Coveralls.

Ladders.

Paint.

I thought that was good, said,

"Good."

He indicated a chart on the wall, said,

"This is your timetable."

"What?"

"Madam likes everything compartmentalized."

It took him awhile to get that last word, but I stayed on and got his drift, said,

"Piecemeal."

He pointed to the chart, said,

"Please examine it."

I did.

> *Monday—Painting*
> *Tuesday—Gutters*
> *Wednesday—Roof*
> *Thursday—Windows*
> *Friday—Patio*

I pretended to be interested, as if it made any sense. I said,

"And Saturday, party down."

He ignored that, said,

"You will arrive promptly at seven thirty. You'll partake of a light breakfast. Work will commence at eight sharp. At eleven you will have a tea break, twenty minutes. At one, you'll have lunch for one hour. You will cease work at four sharp."

I wanted to snap off a Hitler salute, shout,

"Jawohl, Herr Kommandant."

Instead I asked,

"Does she work now?"

"Madam is resting."

"Jeez, from those posters, she's been resting for thirty years."

"She is awaiting the right vehicle."

I nodded at the Rolls-Royce Silver Ghost, said,

"That should do the job."

Any reply he might have made was lost as a van drove up. On the side was

LEE

BUILDING AND MAINTENANCE

An overweight man climbed out. Took him awhile due to the weight he was carrying. He was wearing coveralls and a baseball cap. A dirty baseball cap with LEE barely decipherable.

He ambled over, nodded to Jordan, looked at me, asked, "Who's the douchebag?"

Jordan said, "Mr. Lee, you are no longer employed here. I thought I made that clear."

Lee waved his hand in dismissal, said,

"Lighten up, Jord. The old bat in there doesn't know who's here. I'm not about to let a good thing go."

Jordan sighed, said,

"You have already been replaced, Mr. Lee. I must ask that you leave."

Lee laughed, said,

"You run along, Jord . . . git us a cup o' tea, two sugars. I'll sort out this punk."

Then he moved toward me. Jordan moved faster and delivered two lightning jabs to Lee's stomach. I'd barely time to register it wasn't his fist—open palmed. Lee sank to his eyes, groaning, whined,

"Whatcha do that for?"

Jordan stood over him and, with both hands, slammed Lee's ears.

I said,

"That's gotta hurt."

Then Jordan helped Lee to the van, bundled him in. After a few minutes, the engine turned, and he drove slowly away. Jordan turned back to me, asked,

"Is Monday suitable to begin?"

"You bet."

I lit a roll-up as I walked down the drive. Got to the gate and looked back. The house seemed dead. I began to head for Notting Hill. Halfway down was Lee's van. He was leaning against it, massaging his stomach. As I drew alongside he said,

"I want a word with you, pal."

"OK."

"I didn't get your name."

"No."

He squared up. I noticed his ears were scarlet. He said,

"You don't want to fuck with me, pal."

"Why not?"

"What are you, a smart-ass?"

"A smart-ass with a job—sorry—with *your* job."

He couldn't decide which way to go, settled for verbal, said,

"If you know what's good for you, pal, you'll stay away."

I made a playful feint to his stomach but didn't actually touch him, said,

"You're gonna have to cut down on them burgers, Lee." I walked away. I could hear him muttering the length of Ladbroke Grove. All in all, I kinda liked old Lee. In the rock, they'd have turned him out in a week.

WHEN I GOT BACK to Clapham I could feel the effect Lillian Palmer had on me. I figured it was time I got laid. Went into a phone booth and scanned the cards on display. Every sexual need was catered for. I decided on the following:

TANYA

RECENTLY ARRIVED FROM SOUTH AMERICA

TWENTY YEARS OLD

BEAUTIFUL, BUSTY, READY TO MEET ALL YOUR DESIRES

Yeah.

I rang and set a time. Yup, she could see me now. The address was in Streatham. As I headed there, I swear I felt nervous.

After three years, you wonder how it's gonna be. Found the building and rang the top bell. Got buzzed in, walked up two flights of stairs. Knocked on the door. A guy in his thirties came out. I said,

"Jeez, I hope you're not Tanya."

"Fifty quid in advance."

I paid, and he asked,

"Need anything else—weed, uppers, downers?"

I shook my head. He stepped aside, and I went in. A woman was sitting down, dressed in a slip, stockings and a garter belt. She wasn't in her twenties, or busty or beautiful.

She said,

"Would you like a drink?"

Not South American either. I said,

"Sure."

"Scotch?"

"Lovely."

I watched her as she got the drink. A nice bod—I could feel desire returning. Not wild excitement but getting there.

I took the drink, said,

"Cheers." She stood in front of me, said,

"No kinky stuff, no kissing, no bondage."

What could I say? I said,

"No kidding."

I followed her into the bedroom. The radio was playing the Eagles' "Desperado." If "My Way" is the anthem of chauvinists, then "Desperado" is the rationalization of convicts. She handed me a condom as she lay back on the bed.

It was quick.

She indicated the bathroom, said,

"You can clean up in there."

I did.

When I came out she said,
"For another twenty, we could go again."
I said, "I think I've had as much fun as I can handle."
As I left, she said,
"Call again."

BACK IN CLAPHAM, I went to the Rose and Crown, took a stool at the bar, ordered a pint of bitter. Working on that I rolled a cigarette. A man in his sixties came in and took the stool beside me. I hoped to fuck he wasn't going to be friendly. I fixed my face in the "don't put chat on me" mode. He ordered a large navy rum, said,

"None of that Kiskadee rubbish."

I tuned out. Wanted to engage in some postcoital melancholy.

Then I realized he was talking to me. I said,

"What?"

"Would you believe I was in the middle of an angiogram two months ago?"

"You what?"

"Should have been routine, but an artery the cardio didn't know about got jammed. Just when he's Roto-Rootering another one and—"

I said, "Shut up. I don't wanna hear about it."

He looked wiped, asked,

"Like a drink?"

"I'd like you to bore the ass off someone else."

"Just trying to be friendly."

"I don't do friendly."

Finished my drink and got outta there. When I got outside, a man was standing directly across the road, staring at me. In his thirties, blond hair, a decrepit suit. He looked like he was going to say something, then turned and walked away.

If the traffic hadn't been so heavy I might have gone after him. I thought—"They're coming outta the woodwork today."

THE PHONE was ringing as I got home. Picked it up.

"Mitch?"

"Yeah."

"It's Billy Norton, where've you been—I've been ringing you all morning."

"At a job interview."

"What? You've already got a job."

"Moneylending? That's not a job, it's a virus."

He took a deep breath, said,

"We go tomorrow, like you agreed."

"Yeah."

"Mitch, it's easy, no problem—all you have to do is be my backup."

"Easy? First I heard that taking money was easy."

He was seriously irritated, tried to rein it, said,

"I'll bring some Red Bull."

"Some what?"

"It's an energy drink. You wash down some amphetamines with it, you're seriously cranked."

"Seriously deranged too."

"I'll pick you up at noon, OK?"

"I can hardly wait."

LATER ON, I phoned for a pizza and was waiting for delivery. I was reading Charles Willeford's *Sideswipe* and lamenting there'd be no more of this brilliant series. In prison I'd read one, two books a day. I intended to maintain the habit.

The doorbell went. Opened it. Not the pizza. A well-built man, steel-gray hair, in a dark suit. He asked,

"Mr. Mitchell?"

"Yeah."

He produced a warrant card, said,

"I'm Detective Sergeant Kenny—might I have a word?"

"OK."

He followed me in, examining the room as he did, said, "Nice place."

I nodded. He sat down, said,

"We get a daily bulletin on ex-prisoners returning to our manor."

If he expected an answer I didn't have one.

He took out a packet of cigs, didn't offer, lit up, continued,

"I recognized your name, but hey, no address."

"I'm not on parole, I'm a free man."

"'Course you are. I gave your friend Norton a buzz, and he

was most helpful. So I thought I'd drop by, see how you're set-
tling in."

The doorbell again. This time it was the pizza. Took it and
brought the box in, put it on the table. Kenny said,

"Pizza, great. May I?"

"Sure."

He opened the box, went,

"Mmm, and thank Christ, no anchovies . . . how about a nice
pot o'tea?"

I went and got it going. He shouted in, his mouth full,

"This *is* good. Best to eat it while it's hot."

When I got back with the tea, he'd gotten through half, said,

"God, I needed that, missed lunch."

He sat back, belched. I asked,

"Was there a particular reason for this visit?"

He poured tea, said,

"I had a look at your file. You did three years for aggravated
battery."

"Yeah."

"I was wondering what your plans were now."

"I've got a job."

"By jove! That was quick. Legal, is it?"

"Of course."

He stood up, brushed crumbs off his jacket, said, "Your friend
Norton is sailing close to the wind. You'd be wise to avoid him."

I'd had enough of the bonhomie, asked,

"Is that a threat, Sergeant?"

He smiled, said,

"Whoa, watch that temper, boyo. Wouldn't want to have you in trouble again."

I climbed back, said,

"I'm touched by your concern."

"You will be. Call it intuition."

I went back inside, bundled up the pizza and dumped it in the garbage. He'd put the butt of the cigarette in the dregs of the tea. I said aloud,

"Fucking pig."

NEXT MORNING I was trying to decide what to wear for extortion.

Do you dress up or dress down? Figured I'd play it simple. Jeans and sweatshirt.

Bang on noon, Norton arrived. I got in the van and said,

"Nice day for it."

He was wired to the moon, his foot tapping, fingers drumming on the wheel. As we pulled away, I caught a glimpse of the blond guy in the dead suit, shouted,

"Billy, hold on a mo."

He stopped, and I jumped out. The man was gone. I got back in, and Norton asked,

"What?"

I shook my head, said,

"It's crazy, but I think I'm being stalked."

"You? Jeez, must be a real nutter to stalk you. Here, have a brewski."

There were stacks of cans of Red Bull. I said,

"Naw, I want to do this cold."

He popped a can, drank deep, went,

"Ah . . . r . . . gh."

I asked,

"Did you drop some speed too?"

"Just a half tab, nothing major."

We were roaring down the Clapham Road. I said, "You're sailing close to the wind."

"What?"

"So a policeman told me."

He stared at me. I said,

"Watch the friggin' road."

He shouted, "You spoke to a copper . . . about me?"

"Yeah, the same fuck who got my address from you."

"Oh."

That shut him down for a bit, then,

"Kenny's a jerk-off, you don't need to worry about him."

"He's a jerk-off who knows where I live. That's always worrying."

As we turned into Ashmole Estate, Norton said,

"You've got to lighten up, Mitch; you take things too seriously."

"Right."

I HATE FUCKIN' nuns."

Norton spat this as a nun scuttled along the footpath.

There's a convent in Ashmole Estate. An Estate is what the Americans would call "the projects."

I said, "I thought you Irish had religion."

He grunted, answered,

"What we've got is long memories."

"If you don't have religion, you better have a saving grace."

He gave me the look, said,

"Jeez, Mitch, that's bloody deep."

"But not original. The poet Donald Rawley wrote it."

As we pulled up outside a high-rise, he said,

"I hate fuckin' poets."

We got out, and Norton slung a sports bag over his shoulder, asked,

"You want somefin'?"

"Naw, like I said, I'll go clean."

"I meant protection . . . like a baseball bat. Poems won't cut it where we're going."

"No . . . what's in the sports bag?"

He gave an evil smile, answered,

"Incentives."

THE BUILDING had eighteen stories. An intercom system on the front door, but that had been busted to hell. We pushed through and went to the elevator.

Norton said, "Keep your fingers crossed."

"What?"

"The elevator . . . that it works."

It did.

Covered in graffiti, it smelt of urine and despair. A smell I was familiar with. You don't ever become accustomed.

On the eighteenth, we got out, and Norton said,

"Think of it as golf."

"Golf?"

"Yeah, eighteen holes."

We approached an apartment, and Norton banged on the door. He took out a small red book. The door opened, and a child peered out. Norton said,

"Get your mother."

The mother was Indian and nervous. Norton said, "Dues time."

She went back inside and found a bundle of notes, handed them over. Norton checked his book, counted the notes, said,

"You're a little short."

"It's been a terrible week."

He shushed her, said,

"Hey, I could give a rat's ass, but tell you what, you can double up next week."

She agreed far too readily. The three of us knew she'd never have it.

We went down to the seventeenth, and I asked,

"So how's it work? I mean, it seems to me they just get deeper in the hole."

Norton gave a big smile: all speed and no humor, said,

"See, you're a natural—already you've got the gist. Time comes, they hand over the lease."

"And then?"

"Well, don't you worry none. We have removal specialists."

"So lemme guess. You re-rent."

"Bingo. To yuppies who want a view of the cricket ground. We have six units here already."

The next three floors, it was the same sad story. Pathetic women of all nationalities, promising their lives away. On the twelfth, Norton said,

"I've had nothing but grief from these Spanish twits."

When the door opened, he barged inside. A woman was screaming,

"Nada, nada, nada!"

Norton looked round, asked,

"Where is he, where's your husband?"

The bedroom door burst open, and a man in nothing but bright blue boxer shorts came running out. Brushed by me into the corridor.

Norton was after him like a greyhound, manic smile all over his face.

He was getting off.

He caught the guy at the stairs and jerked the boxer shorts off. With his open hand, he slapped him half a dozen times on the ass.

Then ran him back into the flat. The man was crying, said, "Take the television."

Norton rooted in his sports bag, took out a claw hammer.

Walked over to the TV and smashed the screen to smithereens.

He said,

"Get me the rent agreement."

They did.

Next floor, he said,

"Time out for a break."

Sweat was pouring off him. He was hyped to heaven, said,

"Don't wait to be asked, Mitch; you can jump in at any stage, help me out."

He popped a can of Bull and a tab of speed, asked,

"Do you wanna get laid?"

"Now?"

"Sure, some of them, they'll do you in lieu of the payment."

"I don't think so. Doesn't anyone call the cops?"

"Get real, you think the cops would come to here?"

I rolled a ciggy, lit up, asked,

"The kids . . . doesn't it bother you?"

"So they get to learn early. Toughen 'em up."

He looked with disdain at my roll-up, said,

"You don't have to smoke that shit. You're in a different league now."

I shrugged, said,

"I like 'em."

He took out a pack of Dunhills, luxury blend, got one going, said,

"Can I ask you something?"

"Sure."

He looked round, as if we'd be overheard. The noise in the building was ferocious.

Doors banging

people shouting

kids wailing and

rap music underwrit.

"Prison, what was it like?"

I could have said, "Just like this."

But I was thinking of Tom Kakonis, an American crime writer who understood jail perfectly. He wrote:

> *Call it jungleland, house of mirrors, kingdom of the sociopaths, country of rage, where betrayal is the norm, payback the canon, and mercy never understood or long forgotten. Or, call it a pipe laid across the small of your back, a broom handle up your ass, a shank in your ribs. It means you were utterly alone . . . No one to protect you.*

I didn't tell Norton this; instead I said,

"Mostly, it was boring."

"Yeah?"

"No big deal."

He squashed the can when he'd finished drinking, slung it down the stairs. It hit each step. I could hear it rattling down like a scream on B Wing that lasts until the dawn.

On the ninth floor, we hit turbulence. Norton was doing his number on a black woman when her man came striding out. He swung his fist and caught Norton on the side of the head.

Then he came for me. He was big, strong, but that's all he had.

He wasn't dirty.

I was.

I sidestepped his swing and drop-kicked him in the balls. As he went down, I elbowed him to the back of the head.

Got Norton to his feet, and he wanted to kick the black man till he bled. I pulled him away, said,

"Maybe we'll call it a day."

He agreed, said,

"Nearly through anyway—from eight down it's a bust." Took the elevator the rest of the way. Norton was massaging his head, said,

"I was wrong, what I said about poems."

"Eh?"

"That they're useless. The way you took down that guy, it was fucking poetry."

I headed for the van, and Norton said,

"Come on, there's a pub round the corner, I'll buy you a drink."

At the bar, Norton said,

"We're working guys, let's have a couple of boilermakers."

"Whatever."

The barmaid had to be told it was pints with Scotch chasers.

It was lunchtime, and the special was bangers and mash. It smelled good, almost like comfort.

We grabbed a table at the rear and Norton said,

"*Sláinte.*"

"That too."

On the other side of the Scotch we mellowed out. Norton was counting the cash, writing tallies in his red book. He mouthed the figures as he wrote. Next he put a roll together and snapped a rubber band on it. Pushed it across the table, said,

"Your end."

"Jeez, Billy, I didn't do all that much."

"You will, Mitch, trust me."

WE WERE coming round by the Oval when I spotted the blond-haired man. He was going into the Cricketers. I asked Norton to pull up. He said,

"What's happening?"

"I'm going to stalk a stalker."

"That's supposed to make sense?"

"'Course not."

I got out and crossed the road. Then into the pub. The man was at the counter, his back to me. I walked up, gave him a hearty slap on the back, said,

"Guess who."

He nearly passed out. I noticed he'd a small lager. I gave him a moment to regroup. He said,

"I knew it was a mistake to return."

I took a sip of his drink, said,

"Pure piss."

He looked at the door, and I smiled. He said,

"I'm Anthony Trent."

"You say that like it's supposed to mean something. It don't mean shit to me."

"Oh sorry, of course . . . I lived in the apartment before it became your apartment."

"And now you want . . . what?"

"If I might just collect some things."

I drank some more of his lager, asked,

"Why'd you leave in such a hurry?"

"I got in over my head to Mr. Norton."

"How much is over your head?"

"Ten large."

"So you skipped?"

"Mr. Norton has some heavy friends."

He was staring intently at me, and I said,

"What?"

"I believe you're wearing one of my sweatshirts. Don't tumble dry it."

"Well, Anthony, that's a sad story, but it will get sadder if you follow me again."

"Yes . . . of course, I understand. So might I grab some items from the apartment?"

I took a moment, then said,

"No chance."

THE HOOKER hadn't helped. I couldn't get Lillian Palmer outta my head. I mean . . . what? I fancied an old bird? Get real.

But deny it as I tried, that knowing smile kept returning. She knew I'd been aroused. Each time I blew it off, the wanting to ravish her came pounding back.

I rang Briony, asked if she'd like to come over for dinner. She asked,

"You're cooking?"

"Sure. How does stir-fry sound?"

"Oh Mitch, I'm vegetarian."

Naturally. "How does vegetarian stir-fry sound?"

"Wonderful, Mitch. Shall I bring wine?"

I thought she said "whine." I gave her the address, and she said,

"Poor Mitch, is it a grungy rooming house?"

"Something like that."

"I'll bring flowers, brighten it up."

A thought hit me, and I asked,

"You won't be stealing this stuff . . . will you?"

Silence.

"Bri?"

"I'll be good, Mitch."

"OK."

"Frank likes me to be good."

"Yeah . . . right . . . see you at eight."

* * *

BY THE time eight rolled round, the apartment seemed downright cozy. Pots on the stove, kitchen smells permeating, the table
set. I opened a bottle of wine, poured a glass. It tasted bitter, which
was fine. With booze, I had to keep a tight rein. My jail time was
a direct result of booze.

When I drink whiskey, I get blackouts. I remember the day
clearly. Norton and I had pulled off a caper that netted us three
large ones.

Each.

I was drinking lights out. Even Norton had said,

"Jeez, Mitch, take it easy."

I didn't.

Come that evening, I remember nothing. The story goes that
I got into a dustup with some guy. We took it outside.

Norton followed.

He managed to stop me from killing the guy, but only just.

I got three years.

I'm not arguing the toss. Thing is, my hands were clean.

Not even a grazed knuckle. I mentioned it to my lawyer, who
said,

"You used your feet."

Oh.

MEN FIND all sorts of ways to get through the nights in jail.
Be it

hooch

a bitch

glue.

Me, I worked out all day till my body was exhausted. Some men prayed, if quietly. I took a mantra from Bruce Chatwin's *The Songlines.*

Like this,

"I will see the Buddhist temples of Java. I will sit with sadhus on the ghats of Benares. I will smoke hashish in Kabul and work on a kibbutz."

Mostly it worked.

The doorbell went. I opened it to Bri. She was dressed in a black trouser suit, pink sweatshirt. She handed me a huge bouquet of flowers. I said,

"Come in."

When she saw the place, she went,

"Wow . . . this is great."

I poured her some wine, and she sipped, asked,

"Does wine mix with 'ludes?"

"Ahm . . ."

" 'Cos I wanted to be mellow, not to freak out."

This sounded very promising, if unlikely. She sat down, said,

"I'll move in with you."

"What?"

She laughed out loud. Her laugh was one of the good ones, deep down and only the faintest hint of hysteria. She said,

"Lighten up, Mitch, these are jokes."

"Right."

I went to check on the food, it seemed under control. Bri shouted,

"Sure smells good, Mitch."

I said,

"Should be set in about ten minutes, how'd that be?"

"Lovely."

When I came back, she was arranging the flowers. I sat down, rolled a cig. Bri asked,

"Do I seem different?"

"Ah . . . no . . . you seem . . . fine."

"I've been having therapy."

"That's good, isn't it?"

She put her head down, said,

"I'm not to mention Frank anymore."

I wanted to say, "Thank Christ for that," but what I said was,

"OK."

She did a tour of the apartment, went in the bedroom. I could hear the closet doors opening. When she came back she said,

"You sure landed on your feet, Mitch."

"The crust on its uppers."

"What?"

"It's the title of a Derek Raymond book."

"Who?"

"Never mind."

She poured more wine and pointed to the books, said,

"Will you read all those?"

"I plan to."

Then her face looked sad. I said,

"Bri, I want to read them, I like it."

She was shaking her head, said,

"It's a pity."

"What?"

"You won't have time."

"What are you on about, Bri?"

"At the party, a man said you'd be lucky to last six months."

I tried to lighten it.

"I'll read them easy in six months."

It didn't work.

"I don't want you to go back to prison."

I went and put my arm round her, said,

"Hey, come on, I'm not going back."

"Promise?"

"I promise. I have a regular job."

"I don't do so good without you, Mitch."

"Let's eat . . . what do you say?"

The food was good. I'd done garlic bread and garlic mush-rooms. She liked them best. I opened more wine, and we chowed down. The stir-fry was limp, but it sneaked along. Bri asked,

"What's your job?"

I told her. When I got to Lillian's name, she said,

"I've heard of her. She was the best Blanche DuBois the West End's ever seen."

Every time I had Briony figured, she'd surprise me. I asked,

"How do you know that?"

"I love the theater. Will you sleep with her?"

"What? Jeez, Bri, she's older than me."

Bri looked right at me, asked,

"What does she look like?"

"Well, like Gena Rowlands, not bad at all."

"So you will sleep with her?"

For dessert, there was

Greek yogurt

cheesecake

Black Forest gâteau.

I asked, "Which?"

"All of them."

She wasn't kidding.

After, I went to make coffee. Got that squared away and brought it out on a tray. The tray had Lady Di on the front, and I knew Bri would like that. She was curled up on the sofa, snoring lightly. I picked her up and carried her to my room, covered her with the comforter. I watched her for a bit, then said,

"Sleep precious well."

I decided to leave the dishes. I settled on the couch and turned on the TV, keeping the sound low. It was *NYPD Blue*, and Dennis Franz was massacring a hot dog and a perp simultaneously. Turned it off. I wasn't in the mood for cops. Not even Sipowicz.

About half an hour later, the whiskey came creeping along. Seeping and whispering on the edges of my consciousness. Start now, I'd kill a bottle . . . easy. Jumped up, got my jacket and figured I'd walk it off.

Yeah.

Camus wrote,
    "There is no fate that cannot be surmounted by scorn."

Well, that and a baseball bat should help you on the route from Clapham to the Oval.

What I was thinking was, I'd go see Joe, the *Big Issue* vendor, and shoot the breeze.

At Stockwell, there was a guy holding a placard. He was wearing one of those ankle-length Oz duster coats. They're fine if you've a horse to match. The placard read

DON'T TUMBLE DRY

As I passed, he gave me a huge, toothless grin. I said, "Good advice."

He said, "Fuck off."

When I got to the Oval, no Joe. A kid of about twenty was in his spot and selling the paper. I asked,

"What's happened to Joe?"

"Something should happen," he said.

I grabbed him by his shirt, heard the buttons pop.

I said,

"Don't give me friggin' lip."

"He got hurt."

"What?"

"Straight up, guv, two kids from the Kennington projects done him over."

"Where's he now?"

"St. Thomas's. He's poorly."

I let the kid go, said,

"Don't get comfortable, this is Joe's spot."

The kid was looking at his torn shirt, said,

"Yah tore me shirt, yah didn't have to do that."

"Blame Camus."

"Who's he?"

I flagged a cab and had him take me to the hospital. At reception, I had all sorts of grief before I could locate him. He was on Ward 10. That didn't omen well.

When I got up there, a matron barred my way, saying,

"He's not in any condition for visitors."

A passing doctor stopped, asked,

"What's the problem?"

His name tag read DR. S. PATEL.

The matron told him, and he said,

"Oh yes, the *Big Issue* man. All right, Matron, I'll take care of this."

He turned to me, said,

"Of course, if you're a relative . . ."

"A relative?"

"His brother, say."

I looked into his eyes. I almost never see eyes of kindness.
I did now. I said,

"Sure, I'm his brother."

"Joe is not in good shape."

"You mean . . . he might die?"

"I estimate twenty-four hours."

I put out my hand, said,

"Thank you, Doctor."

"You're welcome."

THE WARD was quiet. Joe's bed was next to the door. So when
they take the remains, it doesn't cause a disturbance. I moved to
the side of the bed. He looked bad. Both his eyes were black-
ened, bruises lined his face and his lips were torn. An IV drip
was attached to his left arm. I took his right hand in mine.

His eyes opened, he said,

"Mitch."

He tried to smile, said,

"You should see the other guy."

"Did you know them?"

"Yeah, two kids from the projects. They're about fifteen . . .
one of them looks like Beckham. Kicks like 'im too. The other
one, he's black."

He closed his eyes, said,

"Jeez, this morphine is a rush."

"Good gear, eh?"

"If I'd that at the Oval, I'd get vendor of the month."

"You will, buddy."

He opened his eyes again, said,

"I don't want to die, Mitch."

"Hey, come on."

"Can I ask you something, Mitch?"

"Anything."

"Don't let 'em cremate me. I don't like fire."

He dozed for a bit.

I pulled over a chair but didn't let go of his hand. My mouth was parched, figured it was the wine.

A nurse came by, asked,

"Can I get you something?"

"A tea, please."

When she came back, she said,

"There's only coffee."

"That's fine, thank you."

It tasted like tea with a hint of castor oil. I'd have killed for a cigarette, but I didn't want to leave. The hours dragged by. He'd wake, see I was there and close his eyes.

About five in the morning, he said,

"Mitch?"

"I'm here, buddy."

"I was dreaming of a red rose . . . what's it mean?"

The fuck I knew. I said,

"That spring's coming."

"I like spring."

Later, he said,

"My feet are so cold."

I moved to the end of the bed, put my hands under the blanket.

His feet were like ice.

I began to massage them and said,

"I'll get yah thermal socks, Joe; be just the job for the Oval."

I dunno how long I was doing the massage when I felt a hand on my shoulder. It was the doctor. He said,

"He's gone."

I stopped rubbing his feet.

Thing is, now they felt warm.

The doctor said, "Come to my office."

I did.

He shut the door, said,

"Smoke if you wish."

"Thanks, I will."

He fumbled papers, said,

"The council will take care of the burial."

"You mean cremation."

"That's the usual."

"I don't think so. I'll make the arrangements."

The doctor shook his head, said,

"Is that wise? I mean, a plot in London is as expensive as a parking space and twice as scarce."

"He's from southeast London, that's where he's going to stay."

"Very well. I'll need you to sign some papers."

I finished my cigarette, said,

"I appreciate all your help."

"You're welcome."

We shook hands. When I got outside, I felt bone weary. Hailed a taxi and had him take me to Clapham. The driver checked me in the mirror, said,

"Rough night, mate?"

"You got that right."

A long time later, I came across a poem by Anne Kennedy, titled "Burial Instructions." Among the lines was "I don't want to be cremated, my clothes sent home in a bag."

As I opened my front door, I smelled home baking. Bri was busy in the kitchen. She shouted,

"Brekky in a moment."

I sank into a chair, beat. I could smell coffee, and it smelt good. Did it ever. Bri brought in a tray. There was

OJ

coffee

toast

brownies.

Brownies?

She pointed at them, asked,

"Know what those are?"

"Ahm . . ."

"Space cookies. Hash cakes. I learnt how to make them in Amsterdam. Eat slow—they tend to blow your mind."

I had some toast, coffee, and considered if I needed my mind blown. I asked,

"Aren't you having some?"

"Oh no, Mitch, they'd mess with my medication."

I thought, "What the hell."

Took a tentative bite. Sweet. Figured, if nothing else, I'd get a sugar rush. Bri asked,

"Were you out robbing?"

"What?"

"Well, I know criminals work at night."

"Jeez, Bri, I'm not a villain . . . I have a straight job."

She wasn't buying this, said,

"I don't mind you being a robber as long as you don't get caught."

I had some more space cake. Bri said,

"Didn't you do villain things before prison?"

No denying that.

As a distraction I told her about Joe, even mentioned the rose.

She asked, "Was he a robber too?"

I near lost it, said,

"What's with this 'robber' shit? Could you please stop using that word?"

"Will I come to the funeral with you?"

"Oh . . . sure. That would be good."

"What will I wear, Mitch?"

"Ahm . . . something black, I guess."

She clapped her hands, said,

"Great, I took a Chanel from Selfridges, but I never got to wear it."

Trying to blunt the sarcasm, I said,

"Took!"

"You told me not to use the word 'robbed.'"

I wolfed the cake.

The bottom dropped out of my mind.

Jazz.

I could hear jazz. Duke Ellington Orchestra with "Satin Doll."

Shit, where did that come from? I knew I wasn't asleep but wasn't conscious either. I tried to move but felt too languid. Vaguely, I was aware of Briony on the edge of my vision, but blurred. Definitely not important. What was vital was I identify the next tune. Yes, Billie Holiday with "Our Love Is Here to Stay." Then the sound track veered and I was Bruce Springsteen with "Darkness on the Edge of Town." Then I was the amp, blowing fit to bust. I felt everything shutting down. I tried to curl into a ball, and then I slept.

Least I think it was sleep.

EARLY MORNING. Norton rang. I asked him to find me a burial plot. In reply he said,

"It will cost. Not just money. I need your help."

"Tell me."

"The Brixton run, none of the lads are keen."

"Gee, collecting money there should be a piece of cake."

"Tomorrow evening, Mitch, I'll pick you up."

WHEN NORTON picked me up the following evening, he was nervous.

I got in the van, and he said,

"I got the grave, here's who you contact."

Gave me a piece of paper, address on it.

"Thanks, Billy, I appreciate it."

I looked round the van, asked,

"No Red Bull?"

"It's not that kind of gig."

"How so?"

"It can get hairy, there's no buzz in it. We go in, get the cash, split."

Brixton was hopping. The streets thronged with people. Seemed almost carnival. I asked,

"Jeez, will anybody be home?"

He nodded grimly.

"Yeah—the women . . . Saturday evening, the men are strutting and the women are glued to the game shows."

We parked near a high-rise off Coldharbour Lane. Norton handed me a sports bag, said,

"Baseball bat. Now, if it gets heavy, run like fuck. Got it?"

"Sure."

We got out, passed a Dumpster and went into the building. The first few apartments went OK. Norton collected at two of them, got rent books in the others. Worked down to the second floor. Norton was as jumpy as a cat. I asked,

"What? It's going good, ain't it?"

He kept looking round, said,

"We're not outta here yet."

Coming out of a second-floor apartment, Norton in the lead, me walking rear. Standing outside were six black men, dressed in black suits, white shirts, spit-shine black shoes. One stood to the front, the others in military line to his rear.

Norton said,

"Fuck."

I asked, "Not good?"

He shouted,

"Run."

And took off like a bat outta hell. I didn't move. Not from bravado but from the look of these guys, they'd have caught me easy.

I let the bat fall, said,

"I'm not going to need it, right, guys?" The leader gave a small smile. I asked,

"Who are you? Nation of Islam?"

I knew the Nation from prison and, more importantly, I knew don't fuck with them.

My final question was,

"It's gonna hurt, yeah?"

The first blow broke my nose. I could describe the beating as

vicious

thorough

brutal.

What it was, was silent. Not a word as they worked me over. Real pros. After they'd finished, they trooped off without a sound. I wanted to shout,

"Is that the best you got?"

But my mouth didn't work. Two of them returned and picked me up, carried me out and threw me in the Dumpster. I lost consciousness for a time. Eventually, I managed to crawl out and fall to the ground. I limped as far as the police station and passed out again. Someone stole my watch before the ambulance came.

I CAME to in St. Thomas's with Dr. Patel standing over me.

Shaking his head, he said,

"What an exciting life you people lead."

God, I felt rough. All my body ached. I asked,

"How bad is it?"

"Your nose is broken, but I think you know that."

I nodded. Big mistake, it hurt like a bastard. He continued,

"Nothing else is broken, but you are covered in bruises. It's almost like whoever did it knew what they were doing. Maximum hurt with minimum breakage."

I asked him to go through my clothes, find the address for Joe's grave. He did. I asked,

"Can you take care of it?"

"Yes, of course."

"When can I get out?"

"You should rest up."

We agreed I could leave in the morning; he'd fit me up with painkillers to get me through the next few days. As I lay there, I realized that Joe was probably still here. At least I was keeping him company. Though not in any fashion I'd have planned.

S UNDAY MORNING, on my way home, I had the cab swing
by the liquor store. I asked,

"Could you get me a bottle of Irish whiskey?" I figured I
could get out of the cab. I wasn't sure I could get back in. He
nodded. As I passed over the cash, he said,

"A bus hit you?"

"A black bus."

"Worst kind. Any particular brand of whiskey?"

"Black Bush."

"Good choice."

He was back in jig time, handed over the bottle, said,

"Get some Epsom salts and a steaming bath."

"I will, thanks."

Back home, I moved like an invalid, dropped some painkillers.
Dr. Patel had warned, "Don't take alcohol with these."

Yeah, right. I unscrewed the bottle, chugged hard. Whoa-
hey, it kicked like a mule. A very bad-tempered mule. I turned
on the radio. Tracy Chapman with "Sorry." Fitting. Ran the bath,
got it scalding. Had some more Bush.

An hour later, glowing from the bath and drink, I wasn't hurting at all. Found a wool bathrobe and wrapped up in that. It had a monogram, but I couldn't focus. The doorbell went. I shuffled over to open it.

Norton, a sheepish face. He went,

"Jesus, what did they do to you?"

"Their worst."

He looked at the bathrobe but didn't comment, asked,

"Can I come in?"

"Why not."

He glanced at the half-empty bottle, said,

"Partying?"

I ignored that, went in and flopped on the sofa. I said,

"There's beer in the fridge."

"Right, think I will."

He popped a can, sat opposite me, said,

"I'm sorry, Mitch. I thought you were behind me."

"I wasn't."

Now he tried indignation.

"What did I tell you? Didn't I say . . . if it gets hairy, run?"

"I musta forgot."

He drank long, said,

"Don't worry, Mitch, we'll get them, eh?"

I was too mellow to be angry. Leave it to a later date. He dropped a chunk of change on the table, said,

"Least you get paid, OK, buddy?"

"OK."

Trying for friendly, he asked,

"So what's this other job you've got?"

I told him the lot, even down to the fast moves of the butler. He said,

"The old dame, sounds like you got the hots for her."

"Don't be daft."

"Tell me again about the Silver Ghost."

Blame the booze, but I did, told him far too much. Should have seen the glint in his eyes. But like I said, my focus was shot to hell. He said,

"Sounds like loot."

"What?"

"Be worth knocking over."

"Hey."

"No, c'mon, Mitch, like the old days. Bound to be a ton of cash jewelry

paintings."

I got to my feet. Not very imposing in the dressing gown, said,

"Billy, forget it. Who d'you think the cops'd pull first?"

"Just a thought. I better get going."

At the door, I said,

"I meant what I said, Billy, stay away from it."

"Sure, Mitch, cross my heart and hope to die."

Back to the couch. I eyed the remainder of the Bush. Sleep took me before I reached for the bottle. I was glad of that when I woke on Monday morning. I felt battered and bedraggled but figured I'd at least show up for work.

The phone rang. Dr. Patel. He'd made the funeral arrangements and wondered about a service. I said no. Joe would be buried on Tuesday evening. I thanked him, and he hung up.

WOULDN'T YOU know, the subway's on the blink, and eventually I had to take the bus. Yet again, Holland Park seemed another world.

As I got to the front door, Jordan opened it. He eyed me with disapproval, asked,

"Accident?"

"Strenuous workout."

"You can't come in here."

"Excuse me?"

"Tradesman's entrance is round the back."

A look passed between us, we filed it for later.

I went round the back into a kitchen. It looked like the one from *The Servant*. I didn't expect, alas, to find Sarah Miles on the kitchen table. Jordan came in, asked,

"Tea . . . coffee?"

"Coffee's good."

He started to arrange filters, and I asked,

"Like real coffee?"

He gave a tight smile, waved to the sideboard, said,

"There's muesli, cornflakes, toast. As you wish."

I nodded. He turned to face me, said,

"Or perhaps you are more accustomed to porridge."

My turn with the tight smile. I asked,

"You're all the staff, then?"

"Madam requires no one else."

The coffee perked. Sure smelled good. One of the disappointments of life, that coffee never tasted as good as the aroma. Took the cup, tasted it, said,

"Shit, that is good."

He held up a finger, said,

"Madam does not allow swearing in the house."

"She can hear us, can she?"

No answer. I took out two painkillers, swallowed them with the coffee. He asked,

"Are you hurt?"

"Like you care."

He left the kitchen. Returned with some packets, said,

"Dissolve one of these in water; they are quite miraculous."

I had nothing to lose, got a glass, tore open one, added water. The powder turned pink. I said,

"Pretty color."

"Madam receives them from Switzerland."

I drank it, tasted sweet but not unpleasant. I said,

"Much as I'd love to chat, I better go to work."

He said, "That's why you're here, isn't it?"

In the garage, I admired the Rolls-Royce again. I'd have given a lot for a spin. Took me awhile to put on the coveralls. My nose was aching like a bitch. I checked the work chart.

Monday—Painting

Okeydokey.

The front of the house, windows and shutters, sure could do with a coat. Got the ladders out and began mixing paint.

Half an hour in, I felt relief. The pain that had been continually battering my body ebbed away. I said aloud,

"God bless Switzerland."

One of the most valuable items in prison is a Walkman. That and a bodyguard. You put those headphones on and slip away. It's not a wise thing to do in the yard. You can't afford to be less than a hundred percent vigilant.

As I leant the ladder against the wall, I put on the Walkman.

The tape was Mary Black. Kicked off with "Still Believing," strange prayers in strange places.

Believe it.

Getting into a rhythm of work, I didn't realize I was at a bedroom window. I could see a four-poster bed. Then she walked into view, wearing a silk dressing gown. I thought,

"Whoops, I better get outta here."

I didn't move. She was taking off the robe. Naked as a jay. Her body was in great shape. I was getting hard. Then she began to dress slowly. Black stockings and silk underwear. She looked up, a tiny smile at the corners of her mouth. I moved down the ladder, my mind on fire. Mary Black was doing "Bright Blue Rose," but I couldn't concentrate. Moved the ladder to another window, got going on that.

I DIDN'T see her for the rest of the day, but she was lodged in my mind like a burning coal. Come lunchtime, I headed for the kitchen. Sandwiches were neatly laid on the table. A bowl of fruit left beside them. There wasn't a sound in the house. So I ate silently and then went outside for a smoke.

Jordan appeared from the front of the house. I said,

"You don't make a lot of noise."

"No, it's not necessary."

Argue that. I didn't.

I thought, "Fuck him," and concentrated on my cig. He was standing watching me. Then,

"You do good work."

"Glad you're pleased."

More silence. I figured I'd let him do the digging. He asked,

"Do you like it here?"

"What? . . . Oh . . . it's different."

"Would you like to move in?"

"Come again?"

"Not in the main house, but there's a room above the garage, a little Spartan but comfortable. TV and shower, of course."

I stood up, asked,

"Are you serious?"

"It would save you commuting."

I didn't want to close any doors. If the Clapham deal went sour, I'd be glad of an alternative. I said,

"Lemme think about it."

As if he read my mind, he said,

"Perhaps, too, you might get to drive the Silver Ghost."

WHEN I got back to Clapham, the Swiss effect had worn off, and I was beat. A BMW was parked outside my place. Tinted windows. The door opened, and Norton got out, said,

"Somebody to meet you."

"Now?"

I couldn't keep the irritation outta my voice. Norton hushed me. I fuckin' love being hushed. He said,

"It's the boss, come to meet you in person."

"Gee whiz."

A large man got out. Wearing a cashmere coat, he had jet black hair, and a pockmarked face and was in his late sixties. An air of casual power. An even larger man got out from the driver's side. Muscle.

Norton said, "Mr. Gant, this is Mitch."

He put out his hand, we shook. He said,

"I've heard a lot about you . . . Mitch."

"Mr. Gant . . . I've heard absolutely nothing about you."

He looked at Norton, then gave a huge laugh. One of those throw-your-head-back efforts, putting lots of teeth in it. Norton said,

"Shall we go inside?"

I opened my door, led them in. Gant took a measured look round, then said,

"You have no answering machine."

"No."

Gant clicked his fingers at Norton, said,

"Take care of it."

I said, "I'm gonna have a brewski. Get you anything?"

Norton and the minder declined. Gant said he'd join me in a beer. I went and got those, took some painkillers. Gant asked,

"May I sit down?"

"Sure."

He took off his coat, rolled up his sleeves. Royal Navy tattoo. Drank the beer from the bottle. Just a working stiff.

I started to roll a cig. He asked,

"Could I have one of those?"

I handed him a rolled one, lit him up. He pulled hard on it, said,

"I don't smoke much, but I tell you, that's the biz."

I nodded, figuring we'd get to the point soon. He asked,

"What tobacco you got there?"

"Golden Virginia, what else?"

Again the fingers snapped at Norton.

"Order up a batch for Mitch."

I realized who Gant reminded me of. In Lawrence Block's Matt Scudder series, there's a character called Mick Ballou. A butcher, he disposes of his enemies without mercy. At the same time, he's a working man who likes nothing better than a drink with the boys.

The mistake is to think he's ever one of them.

Gant leant forward, man-to-man stuff, said,

"You did magnificent at Brixton."

I resisted the impulse to touch my broken nose. He continued,

"It takes some balls to stand up to half a dozen guys."

I tried to look modest. Which is difficult with a beat-up face. He said,

"A man like you sends a message. So I'm going to put a high-rise in Peckham under your control."

I looked at Norton, he was impassive. I said,

86

"I'm very honored, but I'm still learning the ropes. I'd like to tag along with Billy for a bit, learn some more."

He gave a huge smile, said,

"Capital. But I do like to reward industry. I have a special surprise lined up for you, my boy."

"Oh?"

"Free on Wednesday?"

"Sure."

"Splendid. Billy will pick you up around seven. You won't be disappointed."

He stood up, business concluded. At the door, I asked,

"Ever hear of Mick Ballou?"

"Who?"

"A character in a novel."

"I don't do fiction."

And they were gone.

TUESDAY, I was healing gradually. Went to work. I saw neither Jordan nor Lillian. The tradesman's entrance was open and my meals left on the table. I did a good day's work. It was eerie not seeing anybody.

Come lunchtime, I took a stroll down to Notting Hill Gate. I just wanted to see people. Went into the Devonshire and had a half of bitter with a plowman's lunch. Took a window seat, watching the world. A hippie sat opposite me, wearing a T-shirt that said

JOHN LIVES
YOKO SUCKS

He was the Portobello Road variety. Long stringy hair, bad teeth. His brain fried in the sixties, he hadn't touched solid ground since. He had a very battered copy of *Beowulf.*

Gave me the peace sign. Leastways, I took it as such. A pint of Guinness in front of him. He said,

"You're a laborer."

"Shows, huh?"

"The hands, man; good, honest toil."

I figured he'd be a good judge. I nodded. He said,

"Working-class hero, man."

"You think so?"

"Man, John said it all . . . got a smoke?"

Gave him a roll-up, he said,

"Cool."

Time for me to split. I said,

"Stay loose."

"Yo bro, wanna buy a watch?"

"Naw."

"It's a Rolex, man, the real business."

"I'm not into status."

"Me neither, man, but ya gotta try, right?"

I had a lot of replies to that, but what I said was,

"Just . . . *imagine.*"

Made his day.

I FINISHED work at four, still not a soul about. I figured:

   (a) They trusted me.

   (b) They were testing me.

Either way, I stole nothing.

Truth to tell, I sat in the Silver Ghost a bit. Dreamed some crazy dreams. The car smelt of

polished upholstery

oak

old leather

wealth.

As I was walking down the driveway, I turned fast to look at the house. Saw a curtain move in the bedroom window.

That made me smile.

At the Gate I went into Oxfam and found a dark suit. It nearly fit. The volunteer at the register said,

"Oh, that was a lovely find."

"Not really, I was looking for it."

What was lucky was an old Penguin copy of Laurie Lee's *As I Walked Out One Midsummer Morning*.

A guy was selling the *Big Issue* outside Burger King. I got that and said,

"A *Big Issue* vendor is being buried this evening."

"Yeah . . . where?"

"Peckham."

"No can do, mate, too bloody dangerous."

"I think he'd appreciate the effort."

"He's dead, his days of appreciation are over."

I'D BEEN home about twenty minutes, had

a shower

a beer

a painkiller.

Not hurting.

Put on the Oxfam suit. The sleeves were short, the legs too long, but otherwise it fit me like a glove. I got a crisp white Boss shirt from the wardrobe. It fit like a prayer.

Doorbell went.

Briony. She was stunning in a black suit. I said,

"You're stunning."

"I know."

Came in and examined me critically, said,

"You look like an undertaker."

"Thanks, Bri."

She rummaged in her bag, produced a fresh rose, asked,

"Will it do?"

"Perfect."

"Can I have a drink?"

"Sure, whatcha want?"

"Anything lethal, I've only done two 'ludes."

"Black Bush?"

"Lovely."

She clinked her glass against my beer, said,

"To Michael."

"Who?"

"Your friend."

"Joe."

"Are you sure?"

"Trust me, I'm positive."

"OK, to Joe."

We drank. I called a cab, and he came in jig time. A Rasta; the smell of weed in the car was powerful. When I said, "Peckham,"

he said, "Righteous."

The graveyard is at the back of the bus station. Across the road is the bingo hall. I thought Joe would be pleased to hear the call of

FULL HOUSE

The undertaker was waiting. The grave ready, two men standing beside it. No vicar. A man arrived a few minutes later.

"Dr. Patel," I said, "good of you to come," and introduced him to Bri. She held his hand longer than expedient. The undertaker asked,

"Any last words?"

I shook my head. He signaled to the men, and they lowered the coffin. I threw the *Big Issue* in, and Bri dropped the rose. Suddenly, at the gates, a man in full kilt and Scottish regalia appeared—with bagpipes—and began to play "The Lonesome Boatman."

I dunno from beauty, but the piper was beautiful. Bri said,

"A last-minute surprise."

"How did you find him?"

"Outside Selfridges, he does a regular gig."

"Thanks, Bri."

She gave me an enigmatic smile, said,

"Thanks for the doctor."

Uh-oh.

* * *

I PALMED some money to the diggers. One of them said, "Did you know Rod Stewart used to be a gravedigger?"

How do you reply to that? I asked,

"Do you sing?"

"Not a word, mate."

They had a full and familiar laugh. Then I paid the piper, so to speak.

Dr. Patel was deep in conversation with Bri. I said,

"As is usual with a funeral, there's refreshments after. Might I treat you?"

"Yes."

From both.

To get the fuck outta Peckham, we went to the Charlie Chaplin at the Elephant. The best that can be said is . . . it's big.

Bri and the doc took a table, and I went to order.

The barman was a dance short on his card, gushed,

"I love the suit."

"It's been in the family for years."

His eyes lit up, thinking, "A player." He said,

"Don't let it go."

"Never happen."

My wit exhausted, I ordered

toasted sandwiches

hot toddies

beer chasers

potato chips

nuts.

When he finally brought it all to the table, he exclaimed,

"*Voilà!*"

We dug in. No bullshit from the doc. He downed the hot one, chased it with the beer, bit deep into the toasted. Bri went to feed the jukebox, and we were blasted with,

"Hey, if you happen to see the most beautiful girl . . ."

Even I can sing that. I said,

"Doc, you were great to come."

"Please call me Sanji."

"I'll try."

He laughed, then asked,

"Is it terrible to say I'm enjoying myself?"

"It's essential you enjoy yourself."

Bri returned, said,

"That is a happening jukebox." Then she turned to Sanji, asked,

"Were you born in India?"

"Yes. I'm from Goa. Apart from the raves and the hippies, we have the mummified remains of St. Francis Xavier."

Bri and I must have looked blank. He asked,

"You're not Catholics?"

"Not even decent atheists."

He chomped on some peanuts, said,

"His body has been preserved, it's regarded as a miracle."

Having no reply, I made none. He continued,

"Someone stole his toe."

"What?"

"Truly. Someone in the world is a devout believer with the toe of St. Francis."

I couldn't resist, blame the hot toddy, said,

"Isn't that very Catholic, toeing the line?"

He smiled, but I don't think he was amused. Bri excused herself for the ladies'. Sanji gave me an appraising look, asked,

"Might I see . . . your sister?"

Shit.

"I'd advise against it."

"Nevertheless . . ."

"You will anyway. Sanji, you're a good bloke, I like you a lot, but she's not for you."

"Will you let me try?"

"Can I stop you?"

"No."

Bri came back, and Sanji said he'd order another, asked,

"Same of everything?"

"Why not."

Bri leant over to me, said,

"I love him."

"Jesus."

"No . . . really, Mitch, he's like my soul twin."

Out of anger, trying to get her attention, I said,

"What about Frank?"

And got a look of withering scorn. She said,

"Frank's dead, Mitch. The sooner you face up to it, the better for all of us."

Sanji returned, and I felt this was my exit line. I shook his hand and said,

"No doubt I'll be seeing you."

He gave me a concerned look, half medical, half Indian, said,

"I will treat her like a gentleman."

"That's what you think."

As I got to the door, the barman said,

"Yo, party pooper, you can't be leaving already."

"I'm all partied out."

He put his hand on his hip, rolled his eyes, said, "Mmmm . . . tough guy."

Outside, I hailed a cab and resolved next week I'd buy a car.

When I got back to the flat, I wanted to just crash down and out.

Flicked on the TV. Wouldn't you know, just starting was *Point Blank*.

As Lee Marvin appeared in a suit not unlike my own, I said,

"Now, that's a tough guy."

WEDNESDAY WAS RAINED out. I went to work anyway. Jordan was in the kitchen, gave me a critical look, said,

"Your injuries are healing."

"Think so?"

"They appear so."

Zen or what.

Some drains were blocked, and he asked if I could do anything. I said, "Sure."

What a bastard. Took me all day to unclog them. Near four, I was spread out, working on an eave chute, dirty water dribbling in my face, when she appeared. Dressed in a red jersey-knit outfit, it was stuck to her curves. She said,

"Now, that's what I like to see, a man on his back."

I finished the bloody job and got to my feet. She came up to about my shoulder. Again with the knowing smirk. I dunno, was it Joe's funeral, my beating, chemistry, or plain lunacy?

But I grabbed her, pulled her against me and kissed her. First she struggled, but then she blended into me. I got my tongue in her mouth and my hands on her ass, was gone. The rain came bucketing down, and she pulled away, said,

"I hope you can finish what you started."

And she was gone.

I stood in the rain, me and a hard-on, and remembered Wednesday night . . . Mr. Gant's surprise. Back in the garage, I was peeling off the drenched coveralls when Jordan appeared. He said,

"We've gone ahead with the room over the garage. It's all prepared."

"Shit, I dunno."

"There is a shower there, a fresh tracksuit . . . please avail."

I did.

It was a studio-type place:

bed

shower

kitchenette.

And man, bundles of fresh, luxurious towels. As a convict you get a towel per week.

I scalded myself in the shower and, coming out, I noticed a small fridge under the TV packed with beer. I opened a Grolsch and chugged deep.

The bed was freshly made up, and I was sorely tempted. But I had Gant's surprise to come.

The tracksuit was new, black, large size with the logo

COMPLIMENTS OF CLARIDGE'S

Way to go.

On my way out I met Jordan, who said,

"Miss Palmer has expressed a certain . . . *liking* for your . . . work."

"I aim to please."

Blame the Grolsch. He gave a sad smile, said,

"Do aim wisely."

THE NORTHERN Line was up to its usual shenanigans, and I didn't get home till seven. Gant's car was parked outside. The door opened, and Norton said,

"We're late, get in."

The muscle was driving so it was me and Billy in the back. He asked,

"Where the fuck were you?"

"Hey . . . Billy . . . lighten up. I was at work."

He looked at the tracksuit, said,

"You're with Claridge's?"

"Only in an advisory position."

He was very agitated, a light sheen of perspiration on his forehead. He was lighting one cig from another. I asked,

"What's the surprise?"

He muttered, then said grimly,

"You'll fuckin' see."

We drove to New Cross and stopped outside an old warehouse. I asked, "Didn't this used to be the meat rack?"

Norton gave me the look. We got out and went inside. Norton said,

"We're in the basement."

"I didn't know it went below ground."

"There's a lot you fuckin' dunno, mate."

Down he went.

It smelt of rot, piss and desolation. I knew the odor. Below were Gant and two other men. They were standing round a man tied to a chair. A black man. A band of silver tape was round his mouth. Blood leaked from it, so I knew they'd broken his teeth. The southeast London signature.

The black man was wearing a Nike sweatshirt, shot through with sweat. He had Gap khakis that were deep stained from where he'd wet himself. Gant was dressed in a Barbour coat, tan cords. The Browning automatic held loosely at his side was almost incidental. He said,

"Ah Mitch, glad you could join us."

The black man's eyes were huge in his head, locked on mine, they were pleading. Gant said,

"As I mentioned, I do appreciate your lone stand against the . . . protectors. So now, I give you one of them as a mark of my gratitude."

I took a deep breath, said,

"He's not one of them."

Gant near exploded, looked to Norton, to the black man, then slowly back to me. His eyes were black stones. He asked,

"How can you tell? Surely they all look the same?"

"Mr. Gant, when they beat you with total precision, you remember."

He lashed out with his foot and smashed the black man's knee.

Turned to Norton, said,

"You moron, what did you do—grab the first nigger you saw?"

Norton said nothing.

Gant struggled for control, then shrugged, said,

"Oh well."

And shot the black man in the head.

The shot reverberated in the warehouse, and I swear I heard pigeons in startled flight. Gant said,

"So sorry, Mitch, to have wasted your time."

A thousand thoughts were driving in my skull, but I decided to play poker, said,

"All is not lost, Mr. Gant."

He tried to rein in the sarcasm, said,

"Oh really?"

"How would this be? You leave the man in the chair, deliver him as is to the building in Brixton, put a sign on him, let it be."

"A sign?"

"Sure . . . how about:

You borrowed . . .

You pay . . .

back."

A slow smile began on Gant's lips, building to an outright grin. He said,

"Brilliant, I love it. Norton, deliver the goods."

Norton looked extremely pissed off, said,

"Mr. Gant, it could be tricky."

And got the look from Gant.

Gant came over, put his arm round my shoulder, said, "Mr. Mitchell, I may have underestimated you."

I gave my modest look. Then he stood back, said, "Good Lord, I love the tracksuit."

THURSDAY MORNING, I'm heading for work, my nose hurts like a dead horse. I bang refuse to analyze the events of last night.

John del Vecchio, *The 13th Valley*—"It don't mean nothin', drive on."

Pretend as is.

Naturally, there's a line, and everybody's paying with check or card. I don't have a weekly pass 'cos I'm getting a car soon and soonest.

There's an elderly man in front of me, and he's bewildered by the delay. Finally, we get our tickets and head for the turnstile. As we go through, the old man's wallet slips from his pocket.

A fat wallet.

Seen by me and the ticket collector.

There's the moment, hanging for one glorious suspended second as your instincts ride your beliefs. I bend, pick it up, say,

"Sir, I think you dropped this."

The ticket collector and I lock eyes, then he tips his index finger to his cap. The old man is amazed and delighted.

I brush off his gratitude with a shrug. I know myself pretty good. You lie in a bunk bed, twelve hours of lockdown, you see the depths. If the ticket collector hadn't seen it, I'd have kept it, no danger.

I get on the train, settle into a corner seat, am about to hit my

Walkman. I've got Leonard Cohen's "Dance Me to the End of Love" and "Famous Blue Raincoat." Ready to roll.

The old man sits beside me, says,

"I do so awfully hate to intrude, but I am so terribly grateful."

His accent is even plummier than Margaret Thatcher's when she imposed the poll tax. I nod. Encouraged, he says,

"I must tell you a most remarkable story. Apropos what just happened, it has a certain resonance."

Every chancer in London has a story. I just wish they didn't have to tell them on the train. But here he goes.

"I was required to give a urinary sample!"

Here he paused, to check I understood what urine was, then,

"As I had trouble producing at the hospital, they said I might bring it home."

I tried to look like I was hanging on his every word.

"But dear boy, what does one bring it in?"

I could give a fuck, said,

"How complex."

"So I used a naggin' bottle of Johnnie Walker."

If he was expecting praise, I hadn't got it. He continued,

"En route I stopped at the PO to collect my pension."

"Hmmmhh."

"When I emerged, the bottle was gone. What a hoot, eh?"

We'd come to the Embankment, and I had to change for the Circle Line. I said,

"Keep it in your pants, eh?"

He gave a smile, if dubious in its downswing.

I SPENT FRIDAY on the roof; it needed major repair, and I decided to tell Jordan. He said,

"We trust it to see us through another winter."

"Shall I not bother, then?"

He gave me a languid smile, said,

"Fix the most glaring damage, we don't want Madam leaked upon."

I figured I could take that any way I liked. After a day of cosmetic work, I was feeling vertigo. Decided to grab a shower and a brewski. There was no new tracksuit waiting. Thing is, I was a tiny bit disappointed.

My first full week of, if not honest, at least regular work.

Jordan appeared, handed me an envelope, said,

"We presumed you'd prefer cash."

"Good move, Jord."

He didn't go, and I was tempted to say—"Dismissed." What I said was,

"What?"

"Aren't you going to count it?"

"I trust you, pal."

He flicked at a hair on his lapel, said,

"Then you would be making a serious error."

I counted it, went,

"Shit . . . is this for a week or a month?"

He smiled. I wasn't exhilarated, but I was one contented ex-con, said,

"Whatcha say, Jordy, I buy you a large one down at your local."

A beat, then, "I don't fraternize with the help."

I'D HOPED for a glimpse of Lillian, but it wasn't to be. On the train, I considered my plan for the weekend. Nice and simple, find the two fucks who'd kicked Joe to death. Eight that evening, I'd finished a curry and was working my way down a six-pack.

The phone rang.

"Yeah?"

"Mr. Mitchell . . . it's R. Gant—not disturbing you, am I?"

"No, sir, just relaxing.

"Good man, Mitch . . . might I call you that?"

"Sure."

"No ill feelings about last night?"

"No, sir."

"Might I pose you a question?"

I wondered why he was talking like a shithead, but it was his dime. I said,

"Shoot."

A pause, then,

"Jolly good, very timely. My question is this: What do you consider to be the most valuable asset?"

"Jeez, I dunno. Probably money . . . sex . . . digital TV."

"It's power, Mitch, and the most powerful tool is information."

"You're onto something, sir."

Like boring the bejaysus outta me. He said,

"I'd like to share some information with you."

"Yes, sir."

"Not over the phone. I've reserved a table for eight at Browns tomorrow evening."

"Browns?"

"In Covent Garden."

"OK."

And he hung up. All the sir-ing had left a bitter taste in my mouth, and I went to rinse it out. For the life of me, I couldn't think of a single thing he could tell me that I would have the slightest interest in.

SATURDAY MORNING, I woke with a slight curried hangover. Nothing too serious, just hold the red peppers. I thought about Browns.

My kind of place.

Normally, they wouldn't let me in, and I wouldn't blame them. We understood our ratings. To them I was a bottom feeder. But it's a rush sometimes, riding on the clout of a Gant, you get to stray.

Meanwhile, I had business. I knew Joe's assailants were teenagers. One wore a Beckham shirt, one was black. So, Saturday afternoon, they'd be kicking ball.

Dress down.

I wore the faded jeans, unwashed sweatshirt—I was cooking. Got the Glock and dry-fired it. No problem. Loaded it fast. Caught a 36 all the way to the Oval subway station. If I had to describe how I felt, I'd say

certain

and

cold.

Checked out the Kennington projects, quiet yet. OK. I took a walk up to the Walworth Road and did high fives with a gang I once ran with. They lured me into the pub and asked what I'd fancy. I said,

"Bottle of Beck's,"

and jig time, four or five bottles at my hand. They knew I was but recent out, asked,

"How was it—stir and all?"

"Better here."

And got the laudatory salutations.

It was a safe pub. Meaning, the guv'nor had done hard time.

Like eighteen and no remission. So you could talk. Jeff, the organizer of the team, asked,

"Need any cash?"

"Naw, I'm in regular employment."

Huge laugh and four more bottles of Beck's. The team did post offices, usually west or north. They weren't greedy and pulled down a nice earner. I'd served my time with them in my early twenties. Jeff asked,

"We're up north next week, Mitch. Wanna tag along?"

I was tempted. It would be two large, no frills, but alas, I was on a different time frame, said,

"Maybe later."

I hadn't touched one beer. It was getting on to two thirty. I said I had to go, and we did the southeast London trip of truly not-felt good-byes. Outside, for a moment, I wished I could go back.

At the Kennington projects, a furious soccer game was in progress. I sat on the wall, bided my time. Five-a-side, it was deadly serious. I spotted the black kid right off . . . he was a substitute.

A couple of local residents sat alongside me. I passed along cans of lager, get them talking.

Then I saw him, the Beckham shirt and wild, ferocious talent.

Scored a goal from midfield that was beyond description.

Beside me, a man said,

"Aye, he's been scouted."

"Excuse me?"

"Yon kid, he goes up to Middloborough at the beginning of the season."

I said with absolute belief,

"He's very talented."

"Aye, lives to play, take away his soccer ball and he's nowt."

The game wound down after that. I waited. Eventually, the spectators drifted away. But not Beckham. He continued to play, dribble, drive, locked in his soccer dream. The black kid waited, boredom sat large.

Time to rock 'n' roll.

I stood up, stretched, looked round. Deserted. Walking slowly, I approached the Beckham wannabe. He never even saw me. I had the Glock out and pumped both his knees from behind.

Four shots.

Moved straight over to the black kid, whose jaw had literally dropped, stuck the barrel in his mouth, said,

"Not this time, but soon."

Then I walked away. Caught a 3 bus at the ass end of Kennington Park and was over Lambeth Bridge in two minutes.

As we came up to the Embankment, up into Westminster, I let the Hendrix song play in my head, my body drenched in sweat.

"Hey Joe."

I GOT home. I was adrenaline city. Alternating 'twixt a high and cold sweats. Kept thinking—"So, to kill someone, you just aim higher."

Jesus. The rush as I replayed shooting Beckham. So fuckin' easy.

The struggle it had been to stop at four shots. I was only gettin' started. Man, I began to understand the seduction of guns.

Talk about pump city.

Checked my watch, two hours to meeting Gant. I'd have to get a grip, mellow down. Rolled a joint, a big one, muttering, "Camberwell carrot." Cracked a beer and slowed the whole show.

Couple of deep blows, I was chilling.

Went in the shower and took it as cold as I could, shouted,

"Fuck . . . I'm deep frozen here!"

Remembered the first week in prison, when I got the "train," Eight or nine guys putting it in you, blood everywhere and thinking . . . "I'll learn."

As I did.

Came out of the shower, shaking water, shaking memories.

Dress to impress. Yeah.

Put on the Gap khakis, a Boss navy sweater and that blazer.

Thought—"Phil Collins lives."

Ready to roll, I'd just finished the joint when the phone went. Picked it up, said,

"Yeah?"

"Mitch, it's Briony."

"Hi, sis."

"Are you OK?"

"What?"

"You sound odd."

Shit, you spent your day shooting young soccer players, you get to sound odd. I said,

"Was there something?"

I couldn't keep the testiness at bay.

"I'm in love, Mitch."

"Good for you."

"You sound angry, Mitch."

"I'm happy for you, Bri, OK?"

"He gave me three orgasms."

Which was triple the information I needed. I said,

"Oh."

"Are you angry, Mitch? Angry I've betrayed our race?"

"What?"

"I'd have preferred a Caucasian, but it's karma."

I thought of a thousand put-downs but settled for

"Be happy, Bri."

"We'll name our first boy after you."

"Thanks, Bri."

"Love yah."

"Like that."

And she hung up.

In all seriousness, after a call like that, how can you possibly believe life has a purpose?

GOT TO Covent Garden for eight. Browns had a doorman. Before he could start the Nazi spiel, I said,

"Mr. Gant is expecting me."

"Go right in, sir."

Inside, it was plush and Regency. At reception, I did the Gant bit again and was told to proceed to the dining room.

Only a few guests and at the window table the man himself.

He stood up to greet me. Dressed in a gray wool suit, he looked like success. Shook my hand warmly, said,

"Glad you could make it. Tell me, there are two Browns in Covent Garden, how did you know which one?"

"The other has no bouncer."

He gave a quiet laugh, asked,

"A drink before dinner?"

Dennis Lehane has a novel titled *A Drink Before the War.*

I said, "Vodka martini."

Figuring I'd get in the swing of things. The waiter came, and Gant ordered two martinis. Gant was in his early forties; the winter eyes briefly met mine. It was enough. He had arrogance and contempt finely mixed. Plus, he was an ugly bastard. Prison has its share of them . . . they're the wardens.

Drinks came and we sipped. Gant said,

"I'd like you to organize the collections in

Brixton

    Clapham

        Streatham

           and Kennington."

"I dunno, Mr. Gant."

"Call me Rob, eh?"

"OK. Rob."

"You won't have to do door to door anymore. You supervise the teams, make sure they don't skim too much. We all like a little off the top, but no one likes a greedy bugger. Your Mr. Norton, now, he's got way too ambitious."

"Rob, he's my mate."

The waiter brought the menus. Rob said,

"I recommend the lemon sole."

"I think I'll have steak."

"Oh."

We ordered that, and Rob asked for two bottles of wine I couldn't pronounce. The waiter repeated them flawlessly so I'd get the point. The food came, and we piled on veg and potatoes. Rob attacked his with relish, said,

"Really, you should have had the fish."

"In jail, you see a lot of fish."

The waiter was pouring the wine as I said it. Let him get the point. Rob asked,

"Hear about the shooting in Kennington today?"

"No. Missed the news."

"Young soccer player shot."

"If you watched Sky Sports, you'd believe they're not shooting half enough of them."

"Get down that way, do you?"

"Kennington? . . . No . . . not my manor really."

He'd finished his grub and was eyeing mine, said,

"You don't eat like a convict."

"Excuse me?"

"Protectively."

"Not since I read *Miami Blues*."

He ordered dessert: apple tart with two dollops of ice cream. I passed. Finally we got to the coffee, and he lit a cigar, said,

"Feel free to smoke."

I wanted the waiter to see me do a roll-up. Made his miserable evening. Rob said,

"Some habits not covered in that book, eh?"

I didn't feel it needed an answer. He said,

"You'll recall I said information was power."

"Yes."

"In return, I'd like something from you . . . interested?"

"Sure."

He stubbed out the cigar, said,

"You did three years for aggravated battery."

"Yeah."

"You were in a blackout."

"Yeah."

"You didn't do it."

"What?"

"Your friend Norton did the beating."

"That's impossible."

"Were your hands marked?"

"No . . . but."

"Norton's were shredded. The barman followed you out, saw the whole thing. You were too out of it to stand up. Norton legged it, and the cops found you—more coffee?"

"Jesus . . . I . . . no."

"A brandy for the shock."

The waiter brought one of those big bubble glasses. You could wash a shirt in it. He left a bottle of Armagnac on the table.

Rob poured generously.

My mind was spinning. I gulped down the brandy. It burned like pain, gave a solid kick to my heart.

Rob said,

"You'll need time to . . . *digest* the information."

"Why are you telling me?"

Rob considered this, then,

"I could say it's because I like you, but I don't think you'd buy that. Norton has become a major problem. Now he's your problem."

"What if I do nothing?"

He spread his hands on the tablecloth, said,

"Then I'd truly be surprised."

I lit another cig and tried to digest all of this. I asked,

"You said you wanted something from me?"

"Yes. Do you feel my revelation was valuable?"

"That's one word for it. So, whatcha want?"

"A Silver Ghost Rolls-Royce."

I laughed out loud.

"You're kidding. I use the bus, mate."

"But you have access to one."

The penny dropped. I said,

"Norton, the fuck, he told you."

Rob smiled. I asked,

"Why don't you steal it yourself? Shit, you know where it is."

He shook an index finger. I fuckin' loved that. He said,

"You're missing the whole point, Mitch. I want you to steal it for me."

"Why on earth?"

"Let's call it a gesture of good faith."

Rob excused himself to go to the gents'. The waiter was over like a shot, sneered,

"Shall I bring the bill, sir?

"Yeah, and be fucking quick about it."

Rob came back and insisted the meal was on him. I didn't argue. As we were leaving, he touched my arm, said,

"There's no hurry . . . but shall we say delivery in one month?"

Outside, his car was waiting. He said,

"I'd offer you a lift, but like you said, you're a bus person."

"Rob, I don't think I'll be taking up your job offer."

"Well, then, the rent on your apartment is five hundred a week."

"C'mon, Rob."

"Oh, and the other thing, now that we're outside—it's Mr. Gant to you."

With that, he got in the car and was off.

I was going to walk down by Drury Lane but decided I'd had enough theater for one night.

MOVED OUT of Clapham next day. Packed the essentials:

Gun.

Money.

Dope.

I took the Gucci jacket—well, you'd be mad not to. Some sweatshirts and jeans. Left the blazer and dark suit. I didn't plan on any more funerals. A half-dozen crime novels. Was able to fit all that in one bag. Traveling light. Then I just eased on away.

As I walked up the drive in Holland Park, I hoped they'd be home. Went round the tradesman's, entrance. Jordan was at the kitchen table, reading the business section of the *Sunday Times*. If he was surprised to see me, he hid it well, asked,

"You're doing some overtime?"

"Actually, I've come to live with you."

He folded the paper neatly, said,

"Madam was right."

"Yeah?"

"She said you'd move in within a week."

He stood up, said,

"Have some coffee, I'll prepare your room."

I sat down, thinking—"Shit, that was easy."

I was rolling a cig when I remembered the no-smoking rule. Lit up anyway. I lived here. When Jordan returned, he looked at the smoke but let it go. He said,

"I believe all you need is there: shower, hot plate, fridge. There isn't a phone so I've lent you a cell till we get a line in."

I asked, "What's the ground rules?"

"Pardon?"

"C'mon, pal, the do's and don'ts."

He smiled—this guy liked plans—said,

"Very simple. You stay out of the main house unless summoned."

"*Summoned.* I look forward to that."

The summons came quicker than either of us expected. A bell rang, and he said,

"Excuse me."

Ten minutes later he was back, said,

"Madam welcomes you to the Elms and wishes to know if you'd be prepared to drive as part of your duties."

"Sure, do I get to wear a uniform?"

"We don't do uniforms."

I hauled my bag to the garage and went to unpack. The room smelt of air freshener. The cell phone was on the table. A Rolls-Royce in the garage, a cell phone in my hand—welcome to the pleasure dome.

Rang Jeff first, said,

"Jeff, it's Mitch."

"Hi, Mitch, it was good to see you on Saturday. Change your mind about the job?"

"No, mate, thanks. What do you know about a villain named Gant?"

"Whoa . . . bad news, a header to boot, your total fuckin' whacko."

"Oh."

"Your mate Billy Norton runs with 'im."

My mate!

"It's a long shot, Jeff, but would you know where he lives?"

"Yeah, I did a piece of work with him, but never again. Trust me, you don't wanna go there, mate."

"All the same, Jeff?"

"Sure, hang on a mo' . . ."

Then, "Nineteen Regal Gardens, Dulwich. He owns the house and most of the street."

"Thanks, Jeff."

"Give 'im a wide berth, mate."

"I'll try."

Next up I rang Bri, gave her my new address and the cell number. She didn't say anything. I had to ask,

"Bri . . . you there?"

"It's that old girl's address, isn't it?"

"Not like you think, it's work."

"At her age, I'm sure it's very hard work."

And she hung up on me.

Jeez, if Bri wasn't careful, she'd develop a sense of humor.

I was cooking on this cell phone. Rang Norton. Sounded like I woke him. I asked,

"Billy, did I wake you?"

"No . . . I . . . was . . . ahm . . . jerking off. That you, Mitch?"

"Yeah."

"You're fucked, man."

"Excuse me?"

"Gant has a hard-on for you. Oh . . . and you're fired."

"Gee, Billy, you sound broke up about it."

Deep sigh.

"What's with you, man? I get you the sweetest deal, and you shit all over it."

"You're my mate, Billy . . . right?"

"Yeah."

"So lemme tell you, Gant ain't so hot on you either."

"You see . . . you see, Mitch, there you go again, your head's all fucked up."

"Billy, the guy's bad news."

"Mitch . . . you're the bad news. He said you owe him something."

"I owe him jack."

"You better pay it, Mitch, he gets crazy over stuff like that."

"One last thing, Billy. After I did that guy three years ago, how did your hands look?"

Long silence, then,

"You're gone, man, I'm talking to a zero."

And he hung up.

Now I knew it was true. The dirty bastard.

My first year in prison, there was a black queen on the tier above. He'd been turned out his first week and had gone into it wholesale. He was just eighteen and so the legal age for grown-up jail.

He worked at it, trading blow jobs for cosmetics, full anal for lingerie. Every night about eleven thirty he'd begin to sing "Fernando." A slow, crystal-pure version. All blues, all loss.

"Can you hear the drums, Fernando . . ."

For the few minutes of the song, the whole shitty institution went deathly quiet. Not a sound. Just this lone achingly raw lyric.

One evening on chow line, he was ahead of me. I said,

"You have a wonderful voice."

He turned, rouge on his cheeks, eyeliner courtesy of boot polish, said,

"Oh, thank you so much. Do you want a blow job?"

"Naw . . . I just wanted to say you've got real talent."

I was already sorry I'd bothered. Any longer with him and I'd be prey again. I went to move off, he said,

"No . . . you can do me for free."

Jesus.

I dunno why, but I gave it a final shot, said,

"Why do you do . . . that stuff?"

"It's my only protection."

Who was I to argue? I moved off, and the next time he greeted me, I said,

"The fuck you talking to?"

A few months later, he was strangled with a pair of panty hose.

I told myself ignoring him was my protection. Sometimes, I half believed it.

I stood up, threw the cell phone on the bed, said aloud, "Billy-boy, you get to pay for Fernando."

TIME WAS when London was shut on a Sunday. Even the book-ies are open now. I headed into Bayswater and joined the Arab world. If anyone was speaking English, I didn't hear them.

To Whiteleys and found what I wanted on the third floor. In the window was a Silver Ghost, flanked by a Lamborghini and a Ferrari. The salesman approached. I said I'd like the Ghost, and he handed it to me. Perfect in every miniature detail. Not cheap either. While the guy was wrapping it, I spotted a DeLo-rean. The salesman spotted my interest, but I shook my head. I thought—"And they still can't unload one."

Got a small padded envelope and some stamps. Then I ad-dressed the envelope:

ROB GANT

and his home.

I put one stamp on and wrote in glaring capitals:

INSUFFICIENT POSTAGE

Mailed it.

Took a walk in Hyde Park and spent an hour being zoomed by Rollerbladers. Next time I'd take the Glock. Slow down the speed.

I'd no idea what to plan for Norton, figured I'd let it unfold.

Knowing him, he'd make it happen. Gant too, he'd be coming. I could have left London, but where could I go?

Plus, I didn't want to go.

Also, I'd a fix on Lillian Palmer, and I definitely wanted to see where that went. Where else would I get the shot at driving a Ghost?

I went into a café and ordered eggs and bacon. The staff was Thai and friendly to the verge of annoyance. The food was good but tasted slightly of peppers. Shit, what did I know? Maybe they were onto something.

PART TWO
FINAL CURTAIN

I HAD LILLIAN that same night.

Over

under

sideways

on the floor

over a table

on the bed.

Like that.

When we were through, I said,

"I can't understand how you've problems keeping staff."

About eight that evening, I had been lying on my bed, reading one of the John Sandford "Prey" series.

My cell phone went.

It was her. She said,

"I need company."

So I went. Strolled over to the house, all the lights were on. No sign of Jordan. I climbed the stairs. Her bedroom door was ajar, I knocked, heard,

"Enter."

Did I ever.

She was standing by the windows, black silk nightgown.

I walked over, and she asked,

"What kept you?"

Let the frenzy begin. I had three years of prison to vent, and she had her own history.

When finally we were sated, she asked,

"Buck's Fizz?"

"I can only pray you're saying 'buck's.'"

She was. We got through two bottles of Moët, and I finally got to look round the room. In contrast to the rest of the house, it was Spartan. I'd expected hundreds of photos, but not even one. I said,

"How come this room is so . . . empty?"

"One needs an area of simplicity."

"You'd have liked prison."

Then she looked at me, said,

"How the mighty stumble."

I knew this wasn't praise. She asked,

"Do you even know the name of this house?"

"Sure . . . the Elms."

"Its significance?"

"The trees are elms."

"*Desire Under the Elms* . . . Eugene O'Neill."

"Irish, was he?"

She gave a snort of derision.

"My finest role. But I shall yet play Electra."

"You're planning a comeback?"

"Oh yes, I've waited a long time for this. The West End shall hail my return."

"Why now, Lil?"

Her eyes raged, and she tried to slap my face. I caught her wrist, she spat,

"I'm Lillian Palmer, not some bar hussy."

I sat up, said,

"Thanks for the fuck."

She loved that, said,

"Don't go, let me tell you my grand plan."

"I'm sure it's fascinating, but I'm exhausted."

She got up, put on a robe, said,

"They've called me back. Trevor Bailey's office rang three times."

"You'll no doubt tell me who he is."

"*The* impresario. He's producing two shows right now. I want you to drive me there tomorrow, we'll arrive in style."

She went to the bed and, from underneath, produced a huge volume of papers, said,

"It's my work. I've rewritten Electra to make it more modern."

"Nice one."

"I'm giving you the honor of being the first to read it."

Her expression was one of total seriousness. It was her life in those lousy papers. I said,

"I'd be honored."

And she handed them over like a baby. She said,

"We'll do magnificent things, Michael."

I was on the verge of saying Mitchell, but let it go.

On the way down the stairs, Jordan was gliding up. Not a sound.

We didn't speak, nor did he even look at me.

Back in my room, I cracked a brewski, tried to read her work.

It was gibberish. I couldn't follow one single sequence. I slung it on the bed, said,

"Turkey."

I must have been asleep a few hours when the cell phone went.

Jeez, where was the bloody thing . . . found it, muttered,

"Huh."

"Are you finished?"

"What?"

"Were you sleeping?"

"Lillian. No, of course not, I was totally engrossed, lost in it."

I was trying to see the bloody time . . . three fifteen . . . fuck. She said,

"Give me your verdict."

"A masterpiece."

"Isn't it."

"Oh . . . beyond praise."

"Shall I come over, read some now?"

"No . . . no . . . let me just wallow in the magic."

"Good night, *mon cherie*."

"Right."

I've had lots of worry, fear, anxiety in my time, But that I'd *ever* get to see her perform filled me with outright dread.

* * *

NEXT MORNING I headed for the kitchen. Got some coffee and toast going. Already I had the run of the place. Jordan came in and said,

"There are some suits you'll need for driving."

"You have them already?"

Tight smile and said,

"We try to cover contingencies."

I offered him some coffee. Nope . . . unbending, but he stayed, so I asked,

"Have you heard of Bailey?"

"The theater person?"

I was surprised and said,

"So he does exist?"

"Three times he has phoned for Madam."

"You spoke to him?"

"I *always* answer the phone."

I'm on the second toast when he says,

"In regard to Madam's script, I do hope you haven't become a critic."

Steel in his voice, I said,

"No way, pal, I think it's brilliant."

"Good. I wouldn't like Madam to be upset."

"Don't worry."

"Madam wonders if you're free on Wednesday night."

"Free?"

"For bridge."

"Jesus, I don't play bloody bridge."

He gave a long breath of patience,

"We don't expect you to play, merely to accompany Madam when her friends play."

"Sounds like a gas."

The suits got left on my bed. Three of them in

black

gray

blue.

I checked the brand: Jermyn Street. Half a dozen white shirts.

I went to the garage, and the Silver Ghost was shining, waxed and polished. Jordan was standing alongside. I whistled in true admiration, said,

"You did some job, pal."

"Thank you."

"When did you get the time?"

"Last night when you were reading Madam's script."

"Oh."

"I checked with Mr. Bailey's office, and they'll expect you at noon at the Old Vic."

I went upstairs to shower and get those exercises done. Gonna need to be fit for Madam. In the shower, I went,

"What the hell?"

I noticed deep bite marks on my chest. The bloody bitch bit me. Bridge that, Jordan.

There were some old mags on top of the closet. No, not porn. Titles like

GQ

Vanity Fair.

I came across this by Courtney Love:

Fuck all this gender difficulty, fuck all this female experience rage shit. That's Polly Harvey's job.

Now if I could just work this into conversation.

IN THE nick, I came across an old guy who done fifteen hard in Peru. On release, he was deported, and after one week in London he was arrested for robbery. Got seven years.

Said to me,

"I like English prisons, they're kinda cozy."

"Yeah, tell that to the queen who got strangled."

He wasn't listening, away again on his story. Like this:

"First off they strip you and steal anything you have. Then they'd duck your head in a bucket of cold water, put electric wires on your balls. San Juan de Lurigancho—isn't that a lovely name? It was run by the inmates. Cells were sold by the prison mafia. Shit and mosquitos everywhere. But worst is the silence. Silence meant all-out gang warfare."

I could see his point about cozy.

A knock on my door—Jordan.

"Madam is ready."

He'd brought the car round front. She emerged a few minutes later. Dressed in a white linen suit and a fedora. She looked . . . old. I held the door open for her, then went round to the driver's side.

Now I know why people who drive them are arrogant. The damn car makes you superior. As we cruised outta there, I said,

"All right?"

She never spoke the whole way. I could care. The car had my total focus. Thing is too, how could you ever drive anything else? I mean, if I was to get behind the wheel of a banged-up Volvo, was I going to think—"Yup, this is good?"

It sure pulls attention. From admiration through amazement to contempt. A lot of young drivers try to cut you up, but it would take more than a Japanese town car. I was beginning to believe you'd need someone riding shotgun.

We got to the Old Vic, and I pulled in to the side. I said,

"I'll just go and announce you."

"I'll be waiting."

The doorman, a young kid, never heard of her, said,

"Never heard of 'er, mate."

We were arguing when an older man appeared, asked,

"What's going on?"

"I've got Lillian Palmer outside, she's expecting to see Mr. Bailey."

His face lit up,

"Lillian Palmer, my God!"

He went to fetch Bailey. The young guy asked,

"What, is she famous, then?"

"We're about to find out."

A man came striding out, a gaggle of assistants in tow. He looked like an ironed George C. Scott. He had no riding boots or megaphone, but it looked as if he did. He said,

"I'm Bailey."

I told him my story, and he shouted,

"This sounds like Philips's work, get him. Meanwhile, let's meet Miss Lillian Palmer."

He sure knew how to work her. Escorted her by her arm into the theater, led her up onto the stage, turned and said,

"Ladies and gentlemen, fellow thespians, I give you the star."

A spotlight was trained on her, and people flocked round her.

She was transformed, thirty years just vanished from her face. I was thinking,

"Wow, she must have been something."

Bailey must have read my face, answered,

"She was, and a damned fine actress. Is Jordan still around?"

"Yes, he is."

"He was married to her, you know. Hell, at some point, most of us were."

He looked at me, asked,

"Are you drilling there?"

"What?"

"Wouldn't blame you, buddy, she's a class act."

"Did you see her script?"

"At least once a year. Hard to believe it gets worse."

Bailey had champagne and canapés delivered, and they had them on the stage . . . Philips was finally found, and yes, he had rung three times. They wanted to rent the Ghost for promotion. Bailey said,

"In the end, it's all car commercials."

Lillian wasn't told. They followed us to the car, giving her a wonderful send-off.

She was near delirious with joy, said,

"Did you see . . . did you hear? They loved me! I'm going to regain my place. Pull over someplace. I need you to love me."

I pulled over near the north side of Hyde Park. Got in the back and did her as if I meant it. When I got out after, two park keepers gave me a round of applause.

It was a day of performances.

Thursday, back to the day job. Up on that roof, knocking down stray slates. I'd hear them land on the patio, break like glass. If I were fanciful, I'd say like dreams, but they were only worn slates. Madam was on the phone all day, ordering new clothes, the hairdresser, cooing to her friends. I'd yet to meet any of those but figured "bridge night" would answer that.

Come evening, I was showering and resolving I'd get takeout fish and chips and read Edward Bunker. I was holding the new Pelecanos as a special treat. My phone had been installed, and I was settled. Now it rang.

"Mr. Mitchell."

"Hi, Doc."

"How did you know?"

"Doc, have a guess at how many Indians are calling me."

"Oh."

"How'd you get the number?"

"Briony did, she's very resourceful."

"That too . . . so was there something?"

"Yes, could I see you? Let me buy you dinner."

"OK."

"Splendid. There's a wonderful Italian place at Notting Hill, named De Vinci's. Shall we, say eight?"

"Italian?"

"You don't like Italian?"

"Well yeah, sure I do, OK. And call me Mitch."

"Right, Mr. Mitch."

I'd been kinda banking on them fish and chips, but what the hell. I wore the blue suit and a white shirt. Checked myself in the mirror, said,

"Smokin.'"

Wouldn't you know—every one, including the doc, in casual gear.

The place was warm and friendly, and they knew the doc. Good opening. We ordered clams and linguini, then followed with spaghetti bolognese. The bread was crisp and fresh like an idealized childhood. I even liked the wine. I'm mopping up the sauce with that bread, the doc is ordering more wine, and I go,

"What's up, Doc?"

"It's Briony."

"*Quelle surprise.*"

"You speak French?"

"Nope, just that one bit, so I got to ration it. You'd be amazed how often I get to use it with Briony around."

"Can I be honest, Mr. Mitch?"

When you hear that, pay the bill and run. I said,

"Go for it."

"I love her very much."

"But she's a nutter, right?"

That took him aback but also gave him his cue, said,

"When I was a medical student, I seriously considered a career as a psychologist. I learned about borders."

"You mean like perimeters."

"No."

The waiter came and cleared the debris. It was considerable. They like that, like you to eat. Great people. The doc had pavlova for dessert. I settled for cappuccino, without the chocolate sprinkle. I hate that shit. The doc said,

"Essentially they split their feelings from their behavior. The tragedy is, borders never recover. The best you can do is help them coast.

"In the beginning they appear normal, good jobs, but it's a constant tightrope between madness and sanity. Unable to form relationships, never free of a deep rage that leads to self-destruction."

"Her shoplifting?"

"Correct. They live from one disaster to the next. They excel at role-play and have overwhelming feelings of emptiness. They never change."

"Actresses."

"Yes, many borders do well onstage, but then . . ."

I was thinking of Lillian, asked,

"Where's the problem, Doc? Walk away."

He looked down at his dessert, then pushed it from him, said,

"I am besotted with her."

"C'mon, Doc, I'll bring you for a drink in an English pub, if we can find one."

I took him to the Sun in Splendour on Portobello. At least it used to be an English pub. Ordered two best bitters and grabbed a table, said,

"Drink up."

He did. Then gave me a long, analytical stare, asked,

"How can you be so calm . . . about your sister?"

He meant "cold."

That's OK—I can do manners. I said,

"Doc, I've been in prison. I didn't like it at all. I have a strong instinct it's going to require all my energies not to return. I have to play low-key just to survive. I start to burn and I'm a dead man."

He was horrified.

"But it's a terrible existence, such tight control."

I drained my glass, said,

"Beats prison."

After a bit, we had another round, and midway through, he asked,

"What am I to do?"

"Doc, I don't give advice, and I certainly never take it, but lemme say this. Go for it, have a ball, live like fire, 'cause truth is, she'll leave you, she always does. Then she'll resurrect Frank and go back to coke and guns and madness."

"How will I live then?"

I touched his shoulder, said,

"Like the rest of us, pal—the best you can."

THE NEXT TWO weeks were calm. I did my work, read my books, serviced the actress.

I hoped when Gant came, I'd be ready. Else I was fucked.

Chris De Burgh song—"Waiting for the Hurricane." The bridge night proved the dead do return. Three men and a woman. All mummified. You only guessed at them being alive by the cigarettes they smoked.

I didn't play, and no one spoke to me. Except Lillian, who said two things repeatedly:

(1) Another highball, darling

(2) Clean the ashtrays, darling.

Oh yeah, she gave me a present. A silver cigarette case.

I gave it to a wino at Queensway who shouted,

"The fuck is this?"

Exactly.

The change began with a call from the doc, who said,

"She's gone."

"I'm sorry."

"What will I do?"

"Go back to your life."

"What life?"

Welcome to whine city.

END OF two weeks, I was getting restless. That philosopher who said,

"All of man's problems stem from his inability to sit in a room and do nothing."

He was right.

I went down to Finch's on the Brompton Road. On a whim. I had on the Gucci jacket, so I figure it wasn't entirely haphazard. On the train was a discarded copy of the *South London Press*. I read through as the District Line had its usual trauma. I nearly missed it. A small item at the bottom of the page. A man had been found dead outside an apartment building in Clapham. The victim of a mugging. I recognized the man's name and the address.

I was wearing his jacket, I had lived in his home.

In Finch's, I ordered a pint of ordinary, took it to a quiet table. Did a roll-up and wondered was it time for whiskey.

After the *South London Press*, after so much, I was sinking into a nine-yard stare. Didn't even realize, just slipped on back there. I learnt it in prison, or rather, it learnt me. Gradually, I realized someone was talking to me. I refocused, noticed I'd neither touched the drink nor lit the cigarette. A woman at the next table was saying,

"Thought we'd lost you there."

I looked at her, like seriously. In her late thirties, she was wearing a suede tan jacket, black T-shirt and faded-to-comfort jeans. Dark hair, pretty face and a heavy scar under her left eye. I said,

"I was thinking."

"You were comatose."

Irish accent. The soft vowels always distinguishable. Soothing. I took a hefty swallow of the beer, asked,

"Are you trying to chat me up?"

"I dunno. So far, you've had no chat at all."

She was attractive, no doubt, but I hesitated. She said, "There's a lovely word in Irish, it's *brónach* . . . means sadness but a lot more. Anyway, that's how you looked."

And I still couldn't get my mouth in gear. Here's a fine woman, giving it large, and I'm locked in some awful lethargy.

She said, "Your face is a mess, you know. That broken nose, those bruises, is it sore?"

Finally, I said,

"Would you like a drink?"

"No, I'm grand, thanks."

When in doubt, get ugly. It always worked in prison. I asked,

"How come you're on your own in a shitty, pretentious pub north of the river?"

Got her like a slap in the face. She touched the scar, said, "It's that noticeable?"

Relentless, I said,

"Why don't you get it fixed?"

Further slap. She sat back, said,

"I'm sorry I bothered you."

Now I could talk, said,

"I'm Mitch, how you doing? Bear with me, I've had a bad day."

She smiled. God, a smile of such radiance even the scar folded its tent and went away. She said,

"Go on, then, I'll have a half of Guinness."

"Screw that, have a solid drink."

"What's wicked?"

"Whiskey is always wicked."

I ordered two large. Hot so they'd seem tamer. She said,

"God, that's a lovely drink."

I looked at her, asked,

"Do you always say what you feel?"

" 'Course, don't you?"

"Practically never."

HER NAME was Aisling, and once I loosened up, we got on great. I couldn't believe it, I was having me a time. We got out of there, and I had a taxi take us to a club where they play Cajun and serve barbecued ribs to die for. Big buckets of 'em and pitchers of beer. There's no way you can eat them delicately. You get in there, get good and greasy.

She did.

God bless her.

There's a tiny dance floor, and she dragged me on out. The band had a demonic fiddler, and we were possessed. Covered in sweat, we retreated to our table and consumed a pitcher, ate more ribs and were in hog heaven.

She grabbed my hand, said, "Kiss me."

I did, and the menu was complete. Then a guest soloist came on and did a down-home slow rendition of "The Night They Drove Ol' Dixie Down." We danced slow to that, and I came so close to feeling happy.

I nearly got faint. She said,

"You know, Mitch, you're a lovely kisser."

Jesus wept.

She was brushing her hand along the back of my neck, singing along to the song, and my body was electric. She was feeding me the most treacherous poison of all: hope. She said,

"Tell me, Mitch, tell me this place never closes."

"Would it were so."

Then she opened her eyes, said,

"Tell me something lovely; it doesn't have to be true, just some grand thing I'll always remember."

For then, for the moment, I felt she deserved it, I said,

"You're the loveliest person I ever met."

She hugged me real tight, said,

"That's gorgeous and perfect."

It was also true.

Sometimes the gods relent, even they think—"Enough already, let's let the fucker see what it could have been like. As it is for the blessed."

WHEN THE band finished, she said,

"Come back, Mitch, to my awful room in southeast Kensington, and I'll make you Irish coffee."

I did.

We didn't have the coffee, but we did have sweet, gentle love-making like I never believed existed. When I was leaving, she asked,

"Won't I see you again?"

"I hope so, I truly do."

Walked home on air. Cajun tunes, her lilting voice, the sheer softness of her body, bedazzling my mind. Walking up the drive on Holland Park, I muttered,

"Enough of this, I'm outta here."

ON MY pillow was what seemed to be a spider. Black and crushed. I approached slowly and then recognized it for what it was. The misshapen remains of the miniature Rolls-Royce I'd sent to Gant.

I FINALLY BOUGHT a car. Yup, it was time. An old Volvo, worth another six months and no warranty. It was beat up, but who wasn't? Putting her in gear, I banished all thoughts of Royces from my mind.

Took me three nights of cruising to nail Norton. Eventually, outside Biddy Malone's on the Harrow Road. Off his patch.

I waited, as I'd waited the previous nights. Come closing, out he came. High-fiving with the goodnighters.

All the lagered energy of pissed nothing. He was fumbling with the keys to his car, still laughing when I eased the Glock behind his ear, said,

"Who's down in the zero now, shithead?"

Pushed him into the backseat, put the barrel between his eyebrows, said,

"Threaten me now, asshole."

Took him awhile to recover, then,

"Mitch . . . we can work it out . . . yeah?"

"Leaving tokens on my pillow . . ."

"Look, Mitch, can I sit up, please, get us straight?"

I let him and asked,

"Why didn't you toss the room? Among other goodies you'd have found this."

I pushed the barrel against his nose, continued,

"And I'd now be holding my finger up my ass."

Norton shook his head, said,

"He told me to go in quick, not to touch anything. Especially not to let that fuckin' butler see me. He didn't want the surprise ruined."

"What happened to the previous tenant?"

Norton looked at me, asked,

"Heard about that, did ya?"

"*Read* about it."

"Gant couldn't believe you'd gone. We had the place staked, and then that stupid bastard tries to break in. So Gant lost it, you know what he's like, how he did the nigger."

"Then he's still got a hard-on for me?"

Norton gave a harsh laugh, said,

"More than ever. He's in business sometimes with the Co-lombians, and he's in awe of their ruthlessness. They kill every-body that belongs to you."

It took a moment to sink in, then I asked,

"My sister?"

He nodded, said,

"Don't make any new friends."

"What about you, Billy?"

"I'm outta it, soon as I can liquefy my assets, I'm gone."

"Aren't you overlooking your present predicament?"

He looked at the gun, at me, said,

"You're not going to shoot me, Mitch."

I considered it. The bastard of it all was I still kinda liked him. He was garbage, but we had a history, most of it bad but it was there. I said,

"You're right, Billy."

I put the gun away and got out of the car. It was just starting to rain. I turned up the collar of my jacket, and Norton got out of the car. We stood for a moment, then he put out his hand, said,

"Let's shake on it, mate."

"Don't push it."

And I walked away.

I WAS READING Fred Willard's *Down on Ponce*. Right up my street, hard-boiled and hilarious. You've got, like, a guy who describes Atlanta, Georgia, as a city that may be too busy to hate but isn't above taking a little time off to steal.

The phone went. Picked it up, said, "Yeah."

"Mitch, it's Briony."

"Thank Christ, I need to see you."

"I'd like that, Mitch."

"Tomorrow evening, how about I buy you dinner, say that Italian place you like in Camberwell at eight?"

"I'll be on my own, Mitch."

"That's fine."

"I always end up on my own."

"We'll talk about that."

"So you won't bring the old actress."

"No, just you and me."

I hung up, said—"Jesus, she's hard work."

I didn't think I'd be telling her I met someone new. I

certainly wouldn't be telling "the old actress." While I'd been reading, my mind was double-tracking. On the book but also on Gant.

I figured I'd try a temporary solution, rang his number. He answered, and I said,

"Rob, my man."

Silence, then, "Mitchell."

"None other, how are you, bro?"

"Well, Mitchell, I shall be coming to pay you a visit."

"That's why I called. I want to let you know how I've been spending my various salaries. It cost me a few grand, but I've 'engaged' a hitter.

"Here's how it works: You harm me or my sister, he shoots your daughter—what is she now, eleven and doing well at that school in Dulwich, eh? No, there's more. I still had some cash, I could only get a basement deal on your wife. I think it's splendid, how she volunteers for Oxfam those three afternoons. What I got was the 'acid sandwich' for her. See, I took your advice, did my research, like you said . . . information is power."

"You're bluffing."

"That's the beauty of it, you have to decide whether I am or not. Our little variation on *Call My Bluff*. Whatcha think?"

"I think, Mitchell, you have no idea who you're threatening."

"All part of the rush."

"Believe me, Mitchell, we'll be meeting."

"Gotta go . . . oh, one last item. The Nation of Islam is keen to chat with you. About the chap you dropped in Brixton . . . in the chair . . ."

I rang off. It would buy me time. He'd check it out and, sooner or later, he'd come after me. By then, I hoped I'd have come up with a plan. Or at least some more ammunition.

DRIVING TO MEET Briony the next evening, I decided to park at the Oval. Did that and walked over to see how the new *Big Issue* vendor was doing. The kid was there all right and recognized me right off. I bought a copy and felt him eyeing me. I asked,

"How's it going?"

"You did 'em, didn't yah?"

"What?"

"Them young blokes that done Joe—you done 'em."

"The soccer player?"

"Yeah, him who used to wear the Beckham shirt."

"Was he any good?"

"Gifted."

"Well, I'd better be off."

I'd reached my car when the kid shouted,

"You know what I think?"

"Yeah?"

"Fuck 'em."

"Will you keep an eye on the motor?"

"Guaranteed."

I walked down Camberwell New Road. What a shithole. Bad pubs and worse vibes. Young guys in those hooded track-suits cruised continuously. The air was hopping with menace. Like the yard after twelve-hour lockup. Used to be a time, a homeless guy would ask you for a few bob. Now it's demanded. Like this.

A guy clocked me, went by on a first sweep, then back, said, "Gimme a cigarette."

You've got to give it hard and stay on it. Any shit or apology like "I don't smoke" and they'd carve your tongue out.

I said, "Fuck off."

He did.

'Course, if they're cranked, it's a different ball game. There's no rules with a doper. Hurt them fast and keep going. I was deep regretting not driving but all the same, the adrenaline keeps it sharp.

At Camberwell Green, I let out a sigh of relief and went into the restaurant. Briony was already there, working on a glass of wine. She was doing her gothic trip. Dressed in black, white makeup, I said,

"What's this, the banshee look?"

"Do you like it?"

"Awesome."

The owner was an old friend and gave me a high five. Not an easy gesture for an Italian reared in Peckham. I said,

"Good to see you, Alfons."

"And you, my friend. Shall I order for you both?"

"Great."

Briony poured me some wine, we did the "cheers" bit, drank, and I asked, "So?"

"I had to leave my doctor."

"I heard."

"He gave me his pin number."

"That's why you left?"

She laughed. Thank Christ. The evening wouldn't be total gloom. She said,

"I bought a pup."

I thought she said "pub" and went,

"Jeez, how much money had he?"

"A King Charles Cavalier."

"Oh, a pup."

She looked like a little girl—well, a gothic little girl—said,

"He's a King Charles Cavalier."

"Nice."

"They're very docile, like they're on heavy tranquilizers."

"Lucky dog."

Alfons brought the food.

Like this.

The starters: Fritti Misti Vegetable. A selection of zucchini, eggplant, broccoli. Done in a crispy batter.

Crostino al Prosciutto with thinly sliced ham, covered in melting Parmesan cheese.

It was good to watch Bri eat. She did it with delicacy and concentration. She said,

"I called the dog Bartley-Jack."

"Why?"

She looked like she didn't know, said,

"I dunno."

For the main course, Bri had Cotoletta alla Milanese. A beef dish fried with spice in a breadcrumb batter. Melt-in-the-mouth stuff.

I had gnocchi. Small flour dumplings, flavored with porcini. That's a wild Italian mushroom.

I described all of the above to Bri. She was impressed, said,

"How'd you know all this stuff? You hardly speak English most days."

"My first two weeks in prison, before I learnt anything, all I had to read was an Italian menu. It was pinned on the wall of my cell. I must have read it a thousand times. Then someone swiped it."

"Why?"

"It's jail, it's what they do. Doesn't matter what it is."

We had espresso to finish, the burn-the-roof-of-your-mouth, bitter, real thing. I said,

"Bri, I need you to listen seriously to me."

"Sure."

"Is there some place you can go for a while?"

"Why?"

"I have some business to take care of, and I have to not worry about you."

"No."

"What?"

"I have a pup now, I can't just go."

"Jeez, bring the bloody pup with you."

"Not unless you tell me why."

I lit a roll-up, exhaled with a sigh, said,

"There's some people putting pressure on me. They might try to hurt you."

"Hah . . . fuck 'em."

"C'mon, Bri, I'll give you the cash."

"I have tons of money."

"Please, Bri, as a favor to me."

"I might. Why don't you want to know about the doctor?"

"I do really. What happened?"

"He's veggie. A vegan."

"So? Aren't you sometimes that too?"

"I don't like to be told. Anyway, I like villains best, like you."

I gave up. Ordered the bill and paid that. I asked,

"Bri, can I call you a cab?"

"No, I have a bus pass."

"Since when?"

"Like yesterday."

"Take care, hon."

She gave me that smile, promising nothing.

I'd just started back down New Road when a car beeped me.

The window goes down, it's Jeff.

"Mitch, I been looking for you, mate."

"Yeah?"

"Hop in, I'll give you a lift."

"Just to the Oval, I'm parked there."

I get in, and he accelerates. The skels outside just a blur in the speed. He says,

"I need a favor, mate."

"I'll try."

"Monday we go north."

"Yeah?"

"Two of the crew are down. Gerry's gone and broken his leg, Jack's missus is in the hospital."

"Can't you postpone?"

"Last two excursions had to be shelved. It's tough being a villain and a family man."

"And you're asking me what, Jeff?"

"To fill out the crew."

Thing with mates is, you don't make them sweat it.

Yes or no.

I said,

"Yes."

"Oh, cheers, mate. Monday morning at my place . . . eight thirty."

As I got outta the car, he said,

"Be good to have you along, Mitch."

"It's no big thing."

That's what I thought.

AS I walked up the Holland Park drive, I noticed the lights were off. Thank Christ, I thought. Having to hop on the actress was about as appealing as a prison breakfast.

I was about to go to my room when I noticed a light in the kitchen. Thought—"why not?"

Jordan was sitting at the kitchen table in his shirtsleeves, a stone bottle before him. I said,

"Yo."

He looked up, said, "Join me."

" 'Kay."

I'd never seen him without a jacket. I could see his arms were brown, heavily muscled. He motioned for me to get a glass.

I did. He tilted the bottle, poured me a full one, said, "It's jenever, Dutch gin."

We clinked glasses, muttered something that sounded like "skol" and drank them off in one toss. By Jesus, did that kick. A moment of grace, then wallop, your stomach was blitzkrieged. My eyes watered. I gasped,

"Phew."

He nodded, said, "Again?"

"Of course."

After I recovered from the double whammy, I began to roll a cig. He said,

"May I have one?"

"Whoa . . . what about the rules?"

"Fuck them."

I handed him one, lit it, said,

"Now you're talking."

He drew deep, not his first time. Here was a guy reared on smoke. I asked,

"How's Madam?"

"Expecting her call to the theater."

"Jeez! I mean, that ain't going to go down. What then?"

He looked pained. Drunk too, but mainly pained. Said,

"I'll think of something, I always do."

I was feeling the booze, enough to ask,

"What's the deal, why do you stay?"

He seemed amazed, said,

"It's my life."

Didn't elaborate, so I tried more.

"Didn't you used to be her husband?"

My knowing didn't faze him, said,

"I still am."

Then he spread his hands on the table, focused on me.

"Before her I was nothing. She is the beat of my heart."

I figured we were two guys well pissed, so go for it. I asked,

"But . . . doesn't she, you know . . . like, see other guys?"

He spat on the floor, made a sound that went,

"Ph . . . tt . . . h."

Then,

"They are nothing—playthings she discards like rubbish. I am constant."

There was a trace of spittle on his lips, and his eyes were fevered. I considered he might not be playing with a full deck. I eased down, said,

"You sure take care of her."

He waved his hands in dismissal. I downed more gin, asked,

"Ever hear a duet from Garth Brooks and Trisha Yearwood called 'In Another's Eyes?'"

"No."

"Don't listen to music much, eh?"

"There is only Wagner."

I don't think there's a sane reply to this. Leastways, I didn't have it.

Then he did the oddest thing. Stood up, bowed, said,

"I enjoyed our talk, but now I must secure the house."

I got up, not sure should I shake his hand or not. I said, "Thanks for the drink."

I'd just got to the door when he said,

"Mr. Mitchell, if you are ever in trouble, I will be available."

"Oh."

"I am a valuable ally."

As I headed for bed, I didn't doubt that for a minute.

I tried to watch TV for a bit; I was having double vision.

I must have been very drunk, as I thought *Ally McBeal* wasn't bad.

FRIDAY. I figured if I was bank-robbing on Monday, then I better get some R&R.

I phoned Aisling, she said,

"I wasn't expecting to hear from you."

"Why?"

"It's a guy thing. When they say 'I'll call,' you don't hold your breath."

"OK . . . so, can I take you out?"

"Oh yes, I have a plan."

"Nothing better than a plan."

"Can you pick me up at the Angel station at eight?"

"Islington?"

"Is that bad?"

"It's north."

"So?"

"No . . . I can do north."

"See you later."

DID A full day's work:
repaired a door
cleaned the windows
whistled some tunes.

COME EVENING, Jordan laid a wedge of cash on me. He said,
"Madam would like a word."
"Sure, listen . . . I need Monday free."
"Don't make a habit of it."
All the camaraderie of the night before seemed to have evaporated.
But I noticed his eyes were bloodshot. Teach him to guzzle
gin.
Madam was waiting in the dining room. She was looking
good. The battalion of
hairdressers
beauticians
physiotherapists
had done their work. Her skin and eyes glowed. She was

wearing a low-cut cream dress, her skin lightly tanned. Great logo.

I felt stirrings. The body is a bastard, it just does its own thing. Lillian gave the knowing smile, said,

"You must be all hot and sweaty after your toil."

I gave a noncommittal shrug. She said,

"We're going out this evening, I've booked a table at the Savoy."

"Not me, babe."

"Excuse me?"

"I've got other plans."

"Well, cancel them. It's time I was seen in public."

"Have fun, but I won't be with you."

"How do you expect me to appear unaccompanied? I must have an escort."

"Try the yellow pages."

She just couldn't believe I was refusing her, she shouted,

"I will not be denied."

I gave her the hard look, said,

"Jeez, get real, lady,"

and walked out. I could hear her screaming,

"I didn't dismiss you, come back here!"

Jordan, of course, appeared, and before he could speak, I said,

"She's rehearsing, don't disturb her."

As I showered I thought—"She is one royal pain in the ass."

Little did I know.

A FTER I SHOWERED, I cracked a brewski and got dressed. Kept it casual. Sweatshirt and jeans. My nose was still aching, but I could live with it. Gant was hovering on the outskirts of my mind. The mental threads one makes are tenuous and treacherous. I dredged up a line.

It's not about hatred, it's about absolute devastation.

The gems you learn from children's literature. Ready to go, I picked up the cell phone and shoved it in my jeans. The car started on the first turn, and I'd got to the end of the drive when the phone went. I said,

"Yeah?"

It was Lillian, said,

"You are so much more than I had expected but so much less than I had hoped,"

and hung up.

It was ten after eight by the time I got to the Angel station. Islington is a bastard in a car. Aisling was waiting. She was dressed in a duffel coat, faded blue jeans. Looked like a radiant student. I opened the door, she jumped in. Leant over and kissed me on the mouth. I said,

"I'm sorry I'm late."

"We'll be sorry if I'm late."

Let that slide and asked,

"Where to?"

She gave me a complicated set of directions, and I got lost twice. Finally, she shouted,

"Stop!"

I did.

We were parked outside a pub. She said,

"This is Filthy MacNasty's."

"You've got to be kidding."

"No, that's the name."

"Sounds like it should be in the Bronx."

"I remembered you said you love crime writers. Here they have a crime writer read and they play tracks relevant to his work. Guess who's on this evening?"

I had no idea, said,

"I've no idea."

"James Ellroy."

"No shit . . . that's brilliant!"

Already the place was jammed, but we managed to grab two stools at the corner of the bar. Aisling's face was shining, excitement writ huge. She said,

"I'm buying, what would you like?"

"Pint of Guinness."

She ordered that and a Malibu. The drinks came, and we did the "cheers" bit. I asked,

"What's a Malibu?"

"Rum with coconut."

"Good God."

"Try it."

"I don't think so."

"Ah, go on."

I did, went,

"Jesus, paint off a gate, tastes like cough syrup."

She laughed, squeezed my thigh, said,

"I'm delighted to see you."

I felt great. Jeez, when had I ever felt that? She was gorgeous, funny, smart, and liked me. I had money in my wallet and a promising hard-on. Hog heaven.

Then James Ellroy came on. Big guy and wired. He didn't so much read as give a total performance.

Mesmerizing.

When he took a break, he was mobbed. Aisling said,

"Why don't you have a word?"

"Maybe I'll catch him later."

She gave a wicked smile, said,

"Let me tell you about later. I'm going to lure you to my home, fill a bath with

scents

oil

LONDON BOULEVARD

and

you.

"Open a bottle of wine and soak. Then I'll order a huge pizza and eat you while it's hot. Then while you sleep I'll watch over you."

My phone went

I had to squeeze through the crowd to find a quiet spot. A guy muttered,

"Fuckin' yuppie."

Me?

Holding the phone close, I said,

"Yeah?"

"Mr. Mitchell, it's Jordan."

"Yeah?"

"Miss Palmer has attempted suicide."

Oh shit.

"Is she bad?"

"I'm afraid so."

"What can I do?"

"I believe you should come."

"Aw, shit."

"As you wish."

And he hung up. I said,

fuck

fuck

fuck.

A man said, "He reads better after the break."

167

I fought my way back, said to Aisling,

"I gotta go."

"Aw, no."

"Listen, I'll drop you off."

"No, you better get moving."

"Will you be OK?"

"Perhaps I'll have a word with James Ellroy."

"I'll make it up to you."

She gave me a sad smile, said,

"We'll see."

As I left, the sound track was doing U2 with "Sweetest Thing."

Now if that isn't sticking it to you, I dunno what is.

"Jeez," I thought, "where did that come from?"

Maneuvering through the Islington traffic I felt bone weary. Took me near two hours to get back to Holland Park.

Into the kitchen and Jordan was there, I asked,

"How is she?"

"The doctor's given her a sedative, but she's awake."

"Should I go up?"

"Please do."

He had nothing further to add, so I went. Up those stairs like a condemned man. Her bedroom was lit by one bedside lamp. In bed, her arms were lying outside the quilt. I could see the bandages on her wrists. No fuckin' chance she'd cover them.

I said, "Lillian."

"Mitch . . . Mitch, that you, darling?"

"Yes."

She made a grand effort to sit up but then sagged back, whispered,

"I'm sorry, Mitch, I didn't want to be any trouble to you."

I wanted to wallop her, said,

"It's OK, you rest now, everything's fine."

"Is she pretty, Mitch, is she young?"

"What?"

"The girl you're seeing."

"There's nobody . . . I was on a boys' night out."

"Promise me, Mitch, promise you'll never leave me."

My mind was shouting—"How the hell did we get to here?"

I said,

"I promise."

"Hold my hand, darling."

I did. She gave a deep sigh, said,

"I feel so safe now."

I felt exactly like I did when the judge said,

"Three years."

THE WAY TO dress for a robbery is comfortable. It's not the occasion to break in a new pair of shoes. Or to have a pair of briefs mangling your balls.

I arrived at Jeff's place early. Two of the old crew were already there. Bert and Mike, as reliable as concrete. The air was thick with cigarette smoke and the aroma of coffee.

The atmosphere was cranked. These guys were pros, but each time the stakes were rising.

A sofa was littered with weapons. Jeff said,

"We've got a new guy."

I didn't like that, said,

"I don't like that."

Jeff put up his hands, said,

"Me neither, but he's got a rep as a wheelman. We don't got a choice."

Jeff's system was simple. Three cars. One for the robbery, then two changes. These motors had been positioned over the weekend. An expert driver was vital. Jeff asked,

"Want some breakfast, Mitch?"

A huge fry-up was simmering alongside a mountain of toast.

There are two schools of thought on a meal before a caper:

(1) Pig out for the energy level.

(2) Nothing . . . to hike the adrenaline.

I was with the second, said,

"Coffee'd be good."

I moved over to the couch, selected a 9mm, put it in the waistband of my jeans. Took, too, a pump shotgun.

You rack that fucker, you get everybody's attention. Put on a worn combat jacket, packed the pockets with shells. Tasted my coffee, double loaded, it hit like a fist.

KNOCK ON the door, Jeff opened it carefully. Turned to us, said,

"It's the new guy."

A punk came in. Something very familiar about him. He was dressed like Liam Gallagher before he discovered what a gold credit card implied. He had a long gash down the side of his face. I remembered.

At the party, he'd been out back with Briony, and she'd torn his face before putting the gun in his mouth. He said,

"I know you."

I nodded. He smirked, asked,

"How's that crazy bitch sister of yours?"

Jeff intervened, said,

"Whoa, let's all settle down."

I said to Jeff,

"You'll vouch for him?"

"Guaranteed."

I didn't like it, but it was too late to back out. We got organized and headed off. A van was the first leg.

I sat up front with Jeff, the boyos in the back. The punk was mouthing large, but Bert and Mike just ignored him.

Jeff said,

"The target is Newcastle-under-Lyme. The motors are parked at Keele University."

"What's the word?"

"The bank is holding heavy. Maybe twelve thou."

"Nice."

"Let's hope so."

I settled back in my seat, let my mind free-fall.

ONE NIGHT, having serviced the actress, I'd begun to tell her of the range of my reading. I dunno what prompted me to do so, but I was in full flight, listing the different fields I'd read.

When I was done, she said,

"The books of a self-taught man, a working man. We all know how they are,

distressing

egotistic

insistent

raw

striking and ultimately

nauseating."

"You snooty bitch."

She laughed, said,

"Alas, don't blame me, it was Virginia Woolf's analysis of James Joyce. Are you familiar with Virginia?"

"Take a wild guess."

* * *

THE VAN lurched, and Jeff said,

"We're at Keele."

We loaded the gear into the waiting car, got into coveralls.

Bert would remain with the second car and Mike with the third.

It was vital each car be

manned

safe

primed.

The punk got behind the wheel. Jeff beside him and me in back.

As the punk ran through the gears, he said,

"This is a piece of shit."

Jeff said,

"Shut your mouth and drive."

He did.

Twenty minutes later, we rolled into Newcastle. My adrenaline was pumping. Jeff directed the punk to park about twenty yards from the back entrance.

We were out and moving, pulled on ski masks as we hit the entrance. Some firms, they take down a bank, they believe in verbal terror. Go in roaring, screaming obscenities.

Put the fear of God into the citizen; I can see the merits.

But Jeff has his own method. He believes a demonstration is worth a thousand words.

So he shot the first customer we encountered.

S HOT HIM IN the knees. The guy went down. Jeff loaded
his gauge with pellets. Without causing major damage,
they hurt like fuck
look the biz
and scare the bejaysus.

TWO MINUTES, I had staff and customers herded. Jeff went
through the bank like a virus, filled two black bags. Then we
were outta there.

Running for the car, the great British tradition came into
play. Yup, the "have a go" spirit. A guy grabbed me from behind,
clamped his arms round me. The punk was gunning the engine.
I let my body go slack, then with one move stamped my shoe
down on the guy's instep. He let out a roar you'd have heard in
Brixton. Mainly, he let me go. I spun round, stuck the shooter in
his face, shouted,

"Yah stupid bastard, yah want to get killed, is that it?"

Jeff pulled me off, gritted,

"Let's go, c'mon."

Already I could hear sirens. I backed off and ran to the car. We tore outta there. Jeff said,

"Jeez, Mitch, I thought you were going to waste him."

"So did I."

The punk was laughing like a hysteric, said,

"You should 'ave, you should 'ave blown him away!"

If he wasn't driving, I'd have given him a fist up the side of his head.

Got to Keele and switched cars. Then a more sedate pace to the third motor. Changed again, and in jig time we were on the highway, lost in a ton of traffic. Once we got to the van, I let out a long breath. Didn't realize I'd been holding it.

In the back, Mike, Bert and the punk were whooping it up; Jeff was driving and reached under his seat. Pulled out a fifth of Cutty Sark, handed it to me. I drank deep, let it burn. He glanced at me, a grin building. I said,

"Piece of cake, eh?"

BACK AT Jeff's, we began to party. I was drinking Bud and nipping at the Cutty. The punk was doing major damage to a bottle of gin. Jeff and Bert were doing the count.

Mike asked,

"Another Bud, Mitch?"

"Sure."

I was sitting on a kitchen chair, and Mike leant against the table, said,

"You've a hard-on for that kid."

"He's trouble."

"Well, he did OK today."

"See his arms, tracks?"

Mike gave a good look, said,

"Doesn't seem like he's using now, his arms aren't swollen."

"Preparation H."

"What?"

"Takes down the swelling."

Mike was truly surprised, said,

"Jeez, Mitch, how do you know that shit?"

"New Hope for the Dead."

"What?"

"By Charles Willeford."

"You've lost me."

"Lost Charles Willeford too, he's dead, and more's the Irish pity."

Jeff raised his hand, said,

"Yo, people, we've got a tally."

We waited. Then,

"Fifteen large."

Loud yahooing. After Jeff took expenses, we got two-seven each. The punk said,

"Party on."

After a time, the guys began to drift away. Jeff said,

"Got a sec, Mitch?"

"Sure."

When they'd gone, he cracked a beer, said,

"Ever heard of a guy named Kerrkovian?"

"Naw."

"Tall, thin fucker, likes to dress in black. Got eyes like marbles, nothing alive there. I think he's one of those Eastern European gangsters."

"Interesting as it is, Jeff, what's it got to do with me?"

"He's been asking about you."

"Oh."

"Watch your back."

"Yeah. Thanks a lot, Jeff."

"You musta pissed someone off big-time."

"I seem to have a talent for it."

I HEADED for a florist. Ordered up a batch of roses, orchids, tulips. The florist said,

"A mix like that, it's gonna cost."

"Did you hear me bicker?"

"No, but . . ."

Put them in the trunk of the car and headed for Peckham.

Joe's grave was well tended, and a current copy of the *Big Issue*, wrapped in cellophane, rested there. Made me sad.

A man was moving around the cemetery, tidying up. I went over to him, said,

"Hey."

"Hey yourself."

"Did you take care of that grave over there?"

"And what if I did?"

"I just wanted to say thanks."

I peeled off a few notes, and he took them fast. Did wonders for his attitude, said,

"A headstone would make all the difference."

"How would one arrange that?"

He took a flask out of his pocket, offered. I shook my head, and he took a swig, said,

"Keeps the chill off."

"I believe you."

Put the flask away, said,

"If you were to go to your regular stonemason, he'd charge you large. I could get it done for half that."

I peeled off more notes, asked,

"Would you?"

"My pleasure. Want an inscription?"

I thought for a bit, said,

" 'He was the issue.' "

"That's it?"

"Yes."

"You don't want a poem or anything? I've some hot verses in my shed."

"He didn't do poetry."

"Right, I'll get on it."

He counted the money, said,

"There's too much here."

"No . . . keep the extra."

As I headed off he asked,

"How come you trust me?"

"If you can't trust a guy in a graveyard . . ."

He gave a low chuckle, said,

"The biggest rogues are under your feet."

"Words to live by," I said.

BACK AT Holland Park I felt the adrenaline leak away, and I longed for a nap. Jordan came out to meet me, said,

"Madam's been asking for you."

" 'Kay."

"She's not the only one."

"Oh?"

"You had two visitors."

"Together?"

"No, one was a policeman."

"Kenny."

"A bad-mannered individual."

"No argument."

"The other was . . . how do I describe him? . . . In Hungarian, in dialect, there is a word—*Zeitfel*. It means 'a corpse who still walks.' "

"Like a zombie."

"Perhaps. It is fueled by evil, propelled on malice. The Americans have a term: stone killer."

"Was he dressed in black?"

"Yes."

While I digested this, Jordan said,

"As he left, he pointed to the elm."

Jordan nodded to the huge tree to the left of the drive,

"And he said, 'Beware of strange fruit.' "

"Billie Holiday."

"Pardon?"

"She sang a song about a lynched man, called 'Strange Fruit.'"

Jordan reached in his jacket, took out an envelope, said,

"You also got mail."

The handwriting was Briony's. I said,

"Thanks."

I opened Briony's letter. On the front was a sad-looking bear.
He held a sign that read:

I'M SAD

Inside was the following:

Oh Mitch,
   You want me to go away. Christopher Isherwood wrote:
   "Every closet bides the poor little ghost of a stillborn reputation.
Go away, it whispers, go back where you came from. There is no
home here. I was vain and greedy. They flattered me. I failed. You
will fail. Go away."
   Only my little dog loves me.
                    XXX
                    Bri

I guess it would have made more sense if I knew who Isherwood was. Or what his game was.

I lay on the bed and thought about Aisling. I'd really have to
call her. Then I replayed the robbery and the moment when the
idiot grabbed me from behind. For one moment I had truly
wanted to squeeze that trigger.

Had to admit, I'd been amped. I'd gotten off on the rush,
and I just hoped I wouldn't want another fix.

Sleep crept up on me and took me midthought.

I T WAS LATE evening when I woke. A vague sense of foreboding hung over me. I made some coffee, got on the other side of that. Rolled a cigarette and smoked it, sitting on the bed. It tasted as old as I was getting. Showered and put on a crisp white shirt, faded jeans. Checked myself in the mirror. Like George Michael's father before the toilet incident.

The phone went, the actress said,

"I've missed you, Mitchell."

"Well, I'm back."

"I've a special surprise for you."

"I'm dressed for it."

"Pardon?"

"I'm on my way."

"You won't be disappointed."

There was an inch of coffee left in my mug, so I searched out the bottle of Scotch, poured in a generous inch. Balance the books. Took it down fast. What it tasted like was more, but I decided to pace it.

Lillian was waiting in the drawing room. Someone had been

busy, all the furniture was piled at the back. The carpets rolled back. A high gloss on the wood floor. Centerpiece was a small stage, lit by a single spotlight. I thought, "Oh fuck."

One single chair was placed in front of the stage. Beside it was a bureau with a rake of booze. I sat, checked the bottles and saw a Johnnie Walker. Poured a hefty belt. I was going to need it.

Classical music began to play, the lights went down.

Jordan appeared on the stage, dressed in a black suit, dicky bow. He intoned,

"It is my pleasure to herald the return of Lillian Palmer. This evening, she will recite a short piece from D. H. Lawrence. Her lament for an England already lost."

I was feeling lost myself. Gulped down the Scotch. Jordan bowed and withdrew. If he was expecting applause, he'd be waiting.

No sound of one hand clapping.

Then she appeared. Dressed in some kind of flimsy sari. I could clearly see her boobs. Her head lowered. Slowly she began:

> "It is England, my God, it breaks my soul. This England, these shafted windows, the elm trees, the past—the great past, crumbling down, not under the force of the coming birds but under the weight of exhausted leaves. No, I can't bear it. For the winter stretches ahead, where all vision is lost and all memory dies out. I can't bear it, the past, the falling, perishing, crumbling past, so great, so magnificent."

I tuned out. I might even have dozed a bit. Ferocious damage was being done to the Johnnie Walker. Finally, she finished. I stood up unsteadily and shouted,

Bravo.

Magnifique.

Come on, yah Reds.

NEXT THING I know, I'm on the stage and tearing her clothes
off. It was

sweaty

loud

ferocious.

I vaguely recall her sinking her teeth deep in my neck and
me roaring,

"Yah fuckin' vampire!"

After, I lay on my back gasping for breath. She said,

"Am I to believe you appreciated my performance?"

Which one?

I curled up, passed out.

SOMEONE WAS pulling at me, and I was trying to push them
away.

Eventually, I sat up. Jordan was standing over me, said,

"There is something you have to see."

"Now?"

I tried to focus on my watch. Took an effort.

Three forty-five.

"Christ," I groaned, "can't it wait?"

"It's of grave urgency. I'll wait for you in the kitchen."

I shook my head. Big mistake. A mother of a headache. Not

to mention a churning stomach. As Jordan reached the door, he said,

"It might be an idea to put your clothes on."

Aching, I pulled on my jeans and the balled-up white shirt. Then I threw up.

Jordan was holding a flashlight and looked at me. He nodded and headed out. The night was pitch dark. Jordan headed across the lawn and stopped at the elm tree. Waited for me to catch up. He said,

"Are you prepared?"

"For what?"

He shone a powerful beam up into the branches. Billy Norton was hanging from a thick stem. A black, gaping hole where his groin should have been. I muttered,

"Jesus,"

and was on my knees, retching. Jordan switched off the flashlight.

He asked quietly,

"A friend?"

"Yes."

Then he produced a small flask and a pack of cigarettes. Lit one and handed it to me. Then he took the top off the flask and offered it. I drank full, and he said,

"Brandy and port."

When it hit my stomach it thought about regurgitating but opted the other way, settled. I was able to smoke the cigarette.

I avoided looking at Billy. Jordan asked,

"Did you notice his hand?"

"What? . . . No."

"The fingers on the right are gone, it's a signature."

"A what?"

"Vosnok. East European death squad. Since the gates opened, they're unemployed. London attracts the vermin."

"Kerrkovian!"

Jordan nodded, said,

"I trust this is not a police matter?"

"I'd appreciate that."

WE BURIED him behind the house. It was hard work, least it was for me. A hangover doesn't handle well a shovel. Sweat cascaded down my body. Too, I was in my bare feet, and the soil felt like sludge. Jordan dug with an easy rhythm. I said,

"Looks like you've done this before."

"Many times."

I didn't have the nerve to ask if he meant "in this place." Some things you best let slide. When we'd finished, Jordan asked,

"Will you say words for him?"

Part of me wanted to shout—"Good riddance!" I nodded and said,

"Good-bye . . . Billy."

It seemed enough for Jordan. He headed to the house. I followed. In the kitchen I trailed muddy prints and said,

"Sorry."

He produced some of his swiss packets of powder and began to mix that healing elixir. My mind went into free fall.

IN THE joint, you never gave or received favors. It was fraught with peril. I broke that rule only once. For a guy named Craig. I covered his back when he'd lost focus. After, most days he'd chow down with me. Even offered me his dessert.

HIS BROTHER was a cop. Not just any filth but a renowned detective who'd put away more child abusers than Andrew Vachss. But finally, the abyss looked back into him. Drunk one night, he'd found himself cruising for a child. Snapping out of it, he'd gone immediately home and shot himself. Only Craig knew the reason for the suicide. To the cops, he remained a hero and had simply "eaten his gun." Then Craig had looked up from his grub and made full eye contact. Convicts never did that unless they'd a knife or pipe to back it up. He said,

"The point of this story is I avoid zeal. When the gangs go after a chicken hawk here, I abstain."

I got the point. A frenzy had been building in the prison for some days. It usually culminated in a hunt for a sex offender.

I said,

"I hadn't planned on joining the party."

Holding my gaze, he said,

"Self-righteousness is very infectious. People get swept along."

I didn't argue. He was repaying his debt.

Jordan nudged me, handed over a mug, said,
"Drink."

I did.

Jeez, was that the business. Everything near sang, my system felt almost young. He said,

"What will you do about this Kerrkovian?"

"Find him."

"Yes."

I hesitated, but he was prepared to wait. I said,

"Then I'll kill him."

"You'll require assistance."

"It's not your fight."

He folded his arms, said,

"A man comes onto my land, puts a corpse outside my window, and you think I'll turn the other cheek?"

"Who'll mind the actress if we're both gone?"

"I'll make provisions."

I stood up, said,

"OK . . . we'll go hunting."

"Have you a weapon?"

"I do . . . do you?"

He gave me a smile. Humor never entered into it.

I PUT on the radio to ease me into sleep. Dire Straits were doing their riff, the line about Dixie, laden with threat. I hoped Kerr-fuckin-kovian was tuned.

The next day, Jordan ran a test. Using my car. He said,

"I want you to approach the car with suspicion, the backseat you check carefully."

I did. Tried the door, but it wouldn't open. Looked in the window. All I could see was a crumpled blanket on the floor and empty seats. I tapped on the window, the blanket moved, and Jordan unfolded, emerged. I asked,

"How can you make yourself so small?"

He gave a rueful smile, said,

"Years of servitude."

I asked the obvious.

"How come the door won't open?"

"It's an old car, only the front doors open."

"He'll believe that?"

"He better."

It took us three nights to track him. We'd trawled Clapham, Streatham, Stockwell, Kennington and finally got him at a club in Brixton. I'd brought the Glock. I didn't know what Jordan was packing, but I hoped it was heavy. We parked a ways up the road from the club Kerrkovian had entered.

Jordan said,

"Give me the gun."

"What?"

"He'll frisk you."

"Oh."

"I won't wish you luck, as these matters require only timing and nerve."

"I'll settle for luck."

As I got out, I said,

"See you."

"No, you won't."

The bouncer at the door was a grief merchant and intended to give me large, said,

"Members only."

"How much?"

He gave me the calculating look, went with it, said,

"Twenty-five."

I peeled off the notes, asked,

"Don't I get a card or nuttin?"

"I'll remember you."

"Gee, that's reassuring."

I went in. The place was jammed. A Brixton brew of dreads

    goths

        transvestites

           paddies

       minor villains

   bent cops.

I spotted Kerrkovian sitting at a corner table with the punk.
I thought—"Shit."

Moved to them, said,

"Lads."

The punk gave a smirk, said,

"Mitchell."

Kerrkovian was wearing a black suit and looked like a badly
fucked Bryan Ferry. He said,

"I hear many things about you."

His accent was pseudo-American. Like he'd watched all the
very worst B movies. He had rotten teeth—Eastern Europe not
having the best dental plan. He stood up, asked,

"I buy you a brewski?"

"Not right now. I hear you've been looking for me."

"You got it, buddy."

"Well, my car is outside, let's take a ride."

The punk said,

"Get real."

I looked at Kerrkovian, said,

"You wouldn't be afraid to travel with me, would you?"

He smiled, the full frontal of gangrenous molars. I said,

"I'm not packing, you can frisk me."

He did. This was a Brixton club, nobody batted an eye.

The punk said,

"What a jerk-off."

I asked, "So, are you coming?"

"As long as my new friend comes too."

I shrugged. I went first. As we approached the car, I said,

"The back doors don't work."

The punk moved forward, peered in the back windows, said,

"Nothing there."

I got behind the wheel, the punk beside me and Kerrkovian riding shotgun. The punk said,

"Where did you get this heap of shit?"

As I moved to turn the ignition, Jordan was up, had a wire round Kerrkovian's neck. I smashed my elbow into the punk's face, then crashed his head onto the dash. Kerrkovian thrashed and flailed, but Jordan's knee was pivoted against the seat. What seemed like an hour, Kerrkovian went limp, eyes out of their sockets. I said,

"Jordan . . . *Jordan*, you can let go."

"You can never be too careful with this filth."

"Jesus, he's near decapitated."

Jordan let go. I started up the car and got the fuck outta there. Jordan said,

"Go back to Holland Park."

The front seat was awash in blood. Jordan threw the blanket over them. I asked,

"What about this kid?"

"He can help us dig."

Heavy rain began and helped obscure the bundle on the front seat. Blood was leaking over my shoes and across the brake.

By the time we got to Holland Park, the rain was near torrential. I asked,

"What about the actress?"

"She'll sleep till noon."

"You sure?"

"I made sure. Drive up to the garage."

I did.

We got out and inside. Jordan produced rain slickers and said,

"Get the wheelbarrow."

Then we hauled Kerrkovian and the punk into the garage.

The punk was starting to come round. Jordan said,

"Remove everything from their pockets."

From Kerrkovian, I took

a SIG SAUER .45

wallet

cigarettes

stiletto blade and

a piece of paper with a phone number.

It was Gant's.

From the punk, I got

a Browning

thick wad of money

Polo mints

condoms

cocaine.

Jordan filled a bucket of water and threw it over the punk.

He spluttered, choked, then slowly opened his eyes. It must have been nightmarish. Two figures in long waxed coats, the storm and a corpse. He said,

"You broke me nose."

Jordan said, "Stand up, you've work to do."

He got shakily to his feet, whined,

"What's going on?"

Jordan said, "Shut up and you might live."

He shut up.

I asked, "Where are we going to put Kerrkovian?"

"The elm tree, where he placed your friend."

Jordan reached onto a back shelf, produced a bottle of brandy, handed it to me. I drank deep and offered it to the punk.

He was shaking so bad he could hardly hold it. Brandy ran down his front. I said,

"Use both hands."

It made him gag, but he got it down. I passed the bottle to Jordan, who took a small sip. The punk looked to me, said,

"Don't let him kill me, Mr. Mitchell."

Mister!

I said, " 'Course not."

Jordan said, "Help me get the wire out of his throat."

We turned Kerrkovian over, his head was rolling, the teeth had bit clean through his lower lip. The punk went,

"Arg . . . h . . . h,"

and threw up.

The wire had two wooden handles. They looked well worn. I didn't want to think about that. We took a handle each and pulled. It came clear but far from clean. Jordan cleaned it on the dead man's suit. Then he straightened up, cleared his throat and spat on him. He said,

"Lift."

And we threw the body in the barrow. Jordan took the SIG SAUER, hefted it. I said,

"That's the closest thing to a nonjam automatic you'll get."

He pointed it loosely at the punk, said,

"Push that barrow."

The storm had increased. I could feel the rain even through the slicker. The punk had a tough task pushing the barrow, but eventually we got to the elm tree. Jordan threw a shovel on the ground, said,

· "Get digging."

The punk was wiping blood and mucus from his ruined nose, asked,

"By myself?"

"Do it."

The mud made his job a little easier, save he kept slipping.

Jordan handed me a flask, I drank like a demented thing.

Finally, the grave was dug. Jordan leant over the barrow, took a pair of pliers from his coat, cut off Kerrkovian's little finger.

The punk whimpered, and I said,

"Jesus Christ!"

The crack of the bone was like a pistol shot. Then he tilted the barrow, and the body tumbled in. The sound of it hitting was like a splash in hell. Jordan handed me the SIG SAUER.

I said,

"What?"

Jordan looked right into my eyes, said,

"I've noticed your speech is polluted with Americanisms so . . . it's your call."

The punk realized what was going down, pleaded,

"Aw God, Mr. Mitchell, I won't say nuffink."

I shot him in the forehead. He wavered for a moment, then fell into the hole. Jordan picked up the shovel, began to fill the grave. I didn't move, just stood there, rain teeming down, the SIG hanging loose at my side.

Jordan straightened up, said,

"Let's get a cup of tea."

AT THE kitchen table, as Jordan made tea, I said,

"Mickey Spillane always had his characters drink whiskey as he couldn't spell cognac."

He didn't answer.

I didn't care.

He put two steaming mugs of tea down and asked,

"A coobie?"

"Are they Rich Tea?"

"Only Mikado."

"I'll pass, then."

He got a bottle of Glenlivet from under the sink, and I asked,

"What, you have bottles stashed everywhere?"

"Not just bottles."

"Oh."

He unscrewed the cap and dolloped the booze into the tea.

I sipped mine. It tasted like tea with whiskey added.

I rolled a cig and offered it to him. He took it, and I got to work on another. Lit up and we'd a cloud of smoke in jig time. I said,

"Jordan, how'd you get the name? It's not anything to do with basketball . . . is it?"

He sneered, said,

"My father was born on the bank of the Jordan."

"I thought you were Hungarian."

"We moved."

"Did you ever hear the quotation

'I am filled with coffins
like an old cemetery'?"

He stubbed out the butt, said,

"It's not over yet."

"I'm afraid you're right."

I stood up, said,

"I have to get some sleep."

"You'll need it."

PART THREE
ACTS CONCLUDING

JORDAN SENT THE severed finger to Gant.

    Beautifully wrapped.

        Gold box.

            Brittle tissue paper.

                Red velvet bow.

Said to me, "The moving finger having writ . . ."

I said, "You're one sick fucker."

I got back on track with Aisling. She demurred at first, made me sweat it, then agreed. We met at the Sun in Splendour on Portobello . . . I'd bought new shoes. JP Tod's, the real thing. Those suckers are expensive, but wow, are your feet very grateful.

Tan color, I was wearing the Gap khakis with them, a cream sweatshirt and the Gucci jacket. Looked good enough to eat.

Aisling was wearing a killer black dress. I said,

"Killer dress."

She smiled. Things were looking hopeful. She said,

"You're not too bad yourself."

"Do you like the shoes?"

"Bally?"

"No."

"Imitation?"

"Hardly."

"Oh sorry, I forgot you're a man of discernment and taste."

"Isn't that from 'Sympathy for the Devil?'"

"I dunno."

"Before your time, I guess."

She ignored that, asked,

"Where are we going?"

I said, "Fancy dinner?"

"I fancy you, more's the Irish pity."

The thing with the Irish is, they sure can talk, and boy, can they talk well. But what on earth are they talking about?

Fuck knows.

She said,

"Here's a thought, let's rent a vid, order pizza, and you can discover what's under a killer dress."

"Won't it look odd here on the street?"

We went to her place. The minute we got in, she was on me.

Hips grinding, mouth fastened like hope. After we'd done, I gasped,

"What about the pizza?"

LATER WE watched *Three Colors: Red*. I'm not sure I entirely got it. Aisling cried through most of it. I hate fuckin' subtitles. She asked,

"Did you like it?"

"Loved it."

"Truly, you can say, I won't mind."

In the afterglow, I went way over the top, said,

"I love French films, they have a certain . . . *je ne sais quoi*."

She bought it

hook

line

. . . and frenched sinker.

Said, "Oh, I am so happy, Mitch, and you speak French."

The one line I had was from the joint. A serial rapist used to scream it when the vigilantes came for him.

Which they did twice weekly. I said,

"Sure."

She sat up, the sheet falling away from her breasts. I'd have spoken bloody Russian. She said,

"This is so cool, it's part of a trilogy; we can watch *Blue* and *White*."

I nodded, reached for my tobacco and began a roll-up. She watched in fascination. I asked,

"Want one?"

"You're my drug."

Uh . . . huh.

FINALLY GOT to the pizza, blitzed in the microwave. As it dripped down my mouth, Aisling asked,

"All appetites satisfied?"

I nodded.

The radio was playing quietly. They'd been good.

Gram Parsons

Cowboy Junkies

till

Phil Collins began massacring "True Colors."

Aisling asked,

"What are you thinking about?"

I know that answer, said,

"You, dear."

She laughed, and I added,

"We don't need a light, your eyes would brighten any room."

"Shit talk."

The radio kicked in with Iris DeMent—"My father died a year ago today . . ."

Aisling began to cry. I moved to hold her, and she waved me away. Was quiet as the song finished the last haunting melody. She said,

"My dad was an alcoholic. My brother said I lived my childhood like a deer in the headlights of a speeding car. For years the only way I could cope was to move him from the drama to the light entertainment department. When he died roaring from drink, I was glad. At the hospital, they gave me his effects . . . know what they were?"

I had no idea, said,

"I've no idea."

"A Boy Scout belt and rosary beads."

She toyed with a pizza crust, then,

"I threw the beads in the river."

"You kept the belt?"

"It was his estate."

"Jeez, you have a mouth on you, know that?"

She smiled, said,

"You want to hear a crock?"

"A what?"

"A crock of shit."

"Well . . ."

"All you hear nowadays is the New Woman. Doesn't want the traditional things. This woman wants a husband, a home and children."

I kept quiet. Reached for a drink. She said,

"I want you."

Then she leant over, straddled me and began to make love.

I didn't resist. After, she asked,

"Wouldn't I be crazy not to?"

"You would."

I didn't feel crazy. I spent all of the next day with her. Went to Portobello Market, laughed at the junk they were peddling. Drove to the West End and got our photo taken at the Trocadero. Oddly enough, it wasn't a bad snap. Aisling looks young and shining, and me . . . I look like I'm glad she looks like that. I was.

WHEN I got back to Holland Park, it was clocking midnight. The house was dark. I checked on the actress, touched her cheek, she muttered,

"M . . . m . . ."

and continued sleeping.

No sign of Jordan.

Went to my room and cracked a brewski. I had that bone weariness that comes from feeling good. Didn't analyze too closely lest I lose it. Did I love Aisling? Sure as shooting, she made me feel like a person I might once have hoped to be.

Drank the brew, it was cold and satisfying. Got my clothes off and climbed into bed. Jesus, I was beat. Stretched my legs. My toes touched something wet and instantly recoiled. Jumped out of the bed, horror building. Tore back the bedclothes. A ball of blood and gore lay there. My eyes could focus, but the mind wouldn't kick. Had to look closer—it was a dog's head. Briony's dog . . . what the fuck was his name . . . Bartley? Bartley-Jack.

Ever hear Dolores Keane sing "Caledonia?"

I did then.

I dunno why.

As I recoiled from the bed of horror, the song pounded in my head.

Madness, I guess.

Then I felt my shoulders gripped and next a hard slap to my face. I said,

"Hey, easy on the slapping."

Jordan said,

"You were shouting, we don't want to wake Madam."

"God forbid that should happen."

He stepped over to the bed, muttered something in Hungarian.

Something the equivalent of "fuck me." I said,

"It's my sister's dog."

"Why are we still here? Let's go."

We got the rain slickers and the guns, took my car. Traffic was light, and we got across town in about thirty minutes.

Briony lived in a house on the Peckham Road. On a quiet street, just a riot away from the lights.

The house was ablaze with lights. Jordan asked,

"You want front or back?"

"Front."

I kept the Glock in my right-hand pocket. The door was ajar.

I pushed it slowly back. Tiptoed down the hall. Briony was sitting in an armchair, covered in blood. I gasped till I realized it was from the dog, whom she was holding in her lap.

Her eyes were staring, I said,

"Bri?"

"Oh, hello."

I moved into the room, moved near her, asked,

"You OK, hon?"

"Look what they did to my baby."

"Who did?"

"I don't know. When I came home, I found him in my bed. Where is his head, Mitch?"

Jordan stepped into the room. I said,

"Bri, this is my friend Jordan."

"Oh . . . hello, Jordan, would you like tea?"

He shook his head. I said,

"Bri, will you let me hold Bartley-Jack?"

"OK."

I took the mess from her lap. The little dog's body was still warm. That freaked the fuck outta me. Jordan said,

"I'll clean up your sister."

He helped her from the chair and took her by the hand. The phone rang. I picked it up and heard a high-pitched giggle.

I started for the door, and Jordan caught me up, asked,

"Where are you going?"

"It's Gant."

"And?"

"I'm going to kill the fucker."

He turned me round, said,

"Think it through; you want to catch him at a vulnerable time. Has he family?"

"A daughter, school age."

"So, we hit at breakfast."

"After the girl goes to school."

"As you wish."

"How's Briony?"

"She's sleeping, I gave her a sedative."

"What the fuck are you, a mobile pharmacy?"

He smiled. "Among other things."

Jordan went out for about half an hour, returned with a carrier bag, said,

"To help us make it through the night."

"Put a tune to that, you're talking number one with a bullet."

He grimaced. Took out a six-pack of Bud, French bread, ham, tomatoes, pickles, jar of mayo. I asked,

"Where'd you get that shit?"

"This is Peckham."

Argue that.

A few brewskis later, I said,

"Lawrence Block's Matt Scudder said:

> *Winter's no big deal,*
> *dress warm,*
> *walk through it."*

Mid French roll, he asked,

"Which means what?"

"I dunno, seems appropriate."

WE FORMED a plan for hitting Gant's. Rather, we tried various options.

Discarded

modified

arrived at.

Jordan said, "OK. That's good. Now, let's make it look like a drug deal gone sour."

"How?"

He reached in the bag, tossed a

hypo

heroin

and

the works

on the table.

I said, "That's my kit!"

"I know."

I stood up, said,

"You search my room?"

"Daily."

"You fuck, what are you playing at?"

He asked,

"Ever heard of Anthony de Mello? 'Course not. You've read a handful of mediocre crime books and believe you know life."

He didn't say—"You moron!"

But it hung there.

Oh yeah.

He continued,

"De Mello said ninety percent of people are asleep. They never wake up. When was the Hungarian Uprising?"

"What is this, a quiz? What do I give a fuck about the Hungarian Uprising?"

"*Voilà.* You don't even know the basic premise of crime writing. *Cherchez la femme.* I grew up watching men who were decent, compassionate people. They had to hunt down and exterminate the child murderers. In so doing, they had to become the beast, turn to stone. They never smiled."

I had no idea where this was going, said,

"I've no idea where this is going."

He produced some pills from the bag, laid them on the arm of the chair, said,

"De Mello tells the story of the Spanish chicken. An eagle's egg falls into a chicken coop. It hatches, and the chickens raise it as their own. The chick learns to pick at the ground, develops like them. One day, he sees a majestic bird fly over. He's told it is the most superb of all creatures. He returns to pecking at the ground, grows old and dies, believing he's a chicken."

I shrugged, said,

"Very deep."

He didn't answer, so I said,

"Lemme tell you about one of the mediocre crime books I've read. Harry Crews! He wrote 'Comic Southern Gothic'—"

He held up his hand, said,

"You've evidently never heard of the pig."

"What . . . what fuckin' pig?"

"As in . . . don't try to teach a pig to sing. It's a waste of your time, and it only irritates the pig. I apologize for believing you might sing."

Briony cried out, distracting us from where that story might have led us.

She was asleep, but whimpering. I cradled her in my arms and she quietened down. I dozed myself, dreaming of

headless pigs

flying chickens

and

wordless corpses.

Came to as Jordan touched my arm, saying,

"We better go."

He handed me coffee and the pill. I took them. Briony was in a deep sleep, and I kissed her forehead. Jordan was watching us, his expression unreadable.

I said, "Only the dead know Brooklyn."

It was a title by Thomas Boyle. Jordan may not have wanted

to know about crime novels, but it didn't mean he wasn't going to hear it.

We put on the rain slickers, talked quietly about our plan.

The tops of my toes and fingers were tingling. My adrenaline was cranking up a notch. I asked,

"What the fuck's happening to me?"

"You're about to fly."

"What?"

"Let's just say I'm bringing you up to speed."

"Amphetamines?"

"Something like that."

Dawn was breaking. Jordan said,

"I didn't know your sister had a baby."

"She doesn't."

"There's a wardrobe full of baby clothes."

"What? You tossed her room too?"

"Force of habit."

The speed was nipping at my eyes, pushing them wide. Jordan checked his gun, the SIG SAUER. I said,

"You like that number?"

"Nine millimeter, what's not to like?"

We got outside. A street cleaner was leaning against the wall. Smoke break.

A radio was perched on his cart, ABBA doing "I Have a Dream."

He said, "How-ye, men." Irish.

I said, "Nice bit o' weather."

"Least Sky don't own it yet."

Jordan put the car in gear, and we were outta there. I thought about Harry Crews and an interview he'd done with Charlie Bronson. Bronson said,

> *There's no reason not to 'ave friends.*
> *Just the opposite is true. But I don't think you ought to have friends unless you're willing to give them time.*
> *I give time to nobody.*

Got to Gant's home in under twenty minutes. Dare I say, I was speeding. It was just on eight. My system was moving into overdrive. Feet and hands twitching, a flood of fueled ideas toss-tumbling in my head. The street was lined with trees. Jordan said,

"It's a boulevard."

"London's a fuckin' boulevard."

A school bus came slowly down the street. Jordan asked,

"Ever read *Meetings with Remarkable Men?*"

"Desperate men . . . yeah."

He ignored this, eyeing the bus, continued,

"To devour the writings of

     Gurdjieff

         Ouspensky

             Sivananda

             Yogananda

         Blavatsky

     Bailey

. . . Ah . . . and then, to abandon enlightenment, to walk back into darkness."

I was sore tempted to name the Liverpool squad but feared he might shoot me. Gant's front door opened, and a woman emerged, holding a young girl's hand. She fussed with the child's schoolbag, fixed her coat, then gave her a hug. The child boarded the bus. The woman watched the bus leave with an expression of loss. Then she went back inside. Jordan said,

"Let's go."

As we walked, he asked,

"Front or back?" I gave a grim smile, bit down and swallowed hard.

W HAT'S A SOUND TRACK for murder? In my head was
Leonard Cohen's "Famous Blue Raincoat." As I reached
the front door, I muttered about music on Clinton Street. I love
that line.

Rang the doorbell.

Chimes!

Worse, it played a tune . . . "Una Paloma Blanca"! I swear to
God. Just how long had it been since they'd had a vacation?

She opened the door.

I punched her straight in the face. She went back like a sack
of potatoes. I looked round. Half expecting the milkman who'd
say—"She didn't pay you either, eh?"

Took hold of her hair, dragged her inside, shut the door. She
was out cold. A figure appeared in the hallway. Panicked, I
fumbled for my gun. Jordan . . . he shook his head. Then, putting a finger to his lips, he pointed upstairs.

Gant was sitting up in bed, a breakfast tray on his lap. He
looked stunned. I said,

"Mornin', all."

He had a coffee cup en route to his mouth. It was frozen midair. I walked over, slapped it away. Bounced off the wall.

Jordan was standing by the door. I backhanded Gant and said,

"You wanted to see me, eh? Well, here the fuck I am."

He still hadn't spoken. I grabbed him by the pajamas, pulled him from the bed. Jordan took a hammer from his coat and began to smash mirrors. Gant said,

"Aw, c'mon."

I took the Glock out, held it loose, asked,

"When you beheaded the dog, did it make you hot?"

"What?"

I lost it and pistol-whipped him till Jordan caught my arm, said,

"He'll lose consciousness."

Coming out of the speed jag, I saw my arms were splattered in blood. Not mine.

Jordan said,

"Time to go."

Gant managed to focus his good eye, said,

"Let's talk a deal."

I shot him in the mouth. Jordan dumped the drug paraphernalia on the bed, then put a bullet in Gant's head. We did a ransack of the house, turned up

twenty grand

a horde of Krugerrands

three handguns

a stash of coke.

Took it all.

As we prepared to leave, the wife began to come round. Jordan kicked her in the head, asked,

"Want to torch it?"

"No, I hate fires."

As we pulled into Peckham, I said,

"Drop me off here, I want to see a friend."

"Are you sure? I mean, you're flying."

"It's a dead friend."

If he had a reply to this, he didn't voice it. He said,

"All this paraphernalia . . ." He indicated the loot. ". . . is yours."

"What?"

"It's yours."

"You're kidding, shit . . . there's the budget for a small country there."

"I don't need money."

"If you insist."

Blame the speed, but I blurted out,

"I think I'm going to get married."

For the first time I saw Jordan give a look of joy. He took my hand, pumped it warmly, said,

"Wonderful, you're thinking right . . . but I'm not sure if Lillian is actually single."

It took me a moment, then I asked,

"Lillian! Who the fuck's talking about Lillian?"

He dropped my hand, his face clouding, asked,

"Somebody else?"

"Sure."

Then I laughed into a blitz of bullshit about Aisling.

Winding down, I said,

"I'll want you at the wedding . . . OK?"

He opened the car door, said,

"Go see your dead friend."

A T A FLORIST near the bus depot, I bought a shitpile of flowers. I so overdid that the florist began to get nervous. Till I flashed the cash. I was that demented I wanted to tip the guy. Spin a Kruger in the air, say,

"Have yourself a time."

Having invaded a man's house, punched out his wife, dragged him from his bed, then shot him in the mouth, how was I to set the limits?

Thus, I staggered down to the cemetery with the flowers. A guy leaning against the bingo hall said,

"Me oul' flower."

At the cemetery, the caretaker had placed a white cross on Joe's grave. I said,

"Hey, Joe."

Laid the flowers carefully down. I stood there, up to my eyes in death. I told Joe what had been happening. Then I said,

"I miss you, man."

Back at Holland Park, the speed had evaporated, and I was having a killer downer. I sat on the bed, drank some

Scotch, tried to ease the blues. On the bed were the spoils. I said aloud,

"I'm rich, then . . . aren't I . . . fuckin' rich."

The phone rang.

Lillian.

She purred, "How are you, darling?"

"I'm beat is what I am."

"You rest, lover, we'll love later."

"Sure."

"Everything's taken care of now, darling."

"Is it?"

"Oh yes, sleep, my sweet."

I lay on the bed and thought—"What am I missing here?"

I RODE the actress as if I meant it. She was surprised at my energy, said,

"Who's been taking their vitamins?"

Sickening myself, I said,

"There's more where that came from."

She hugged me close. I felt postcoital repulsion. I'd made up my mind, one week and I'd walk. Set up home with Aisling and chill. Lillian said,

"Did you see a set of keys on the table?"

"No."

"Go see."

"Now?"

"Please, darling."

I got up, walked naked to the table. A set of shiny keys, picked them up. I could feel Lillian's eyes burn along my body. Went back to the bed, asked,

"These them?"

Her face was glowing, she said,

"They're for a BMW."

"Nice."

"Your BMW."

"What?"

"Took delivery today. I hope you like red."

I hate fucking red, said,

"My favorite."

"Oh darling, it's just the beginning, I'm going to spoil you silly."

"You don't need to do that."

"I want to."

She lay back, and I knew I'd those keys to earn.

I was coming down the stairs as Jordan was coming up. He was holding a silver tray, piled high with letters. I said,

"Bills, eh?"

"Fan mail."

"What?"

"Every day, she hears from her public."

"What makes you so sure they're fan letters?"

"I write them."

The following evening, I was to call at Aisling's place. She'd promised me "an Oirish night."

"What's that?"

"Well, you get to

drink Black Velvet

eat Irish stew

listen to Clannad

and

bed a colleen."

"Sounds great."

"It is."

IN THE afternoon, I went shopping. Time to burn some of the cash. First off to the city. There's a jeweler's tucked right in the center. Chris Brady, the proprietor, and I go way back. He has an Errol Flynn look. Buckets of charm and graceful movement. He recommends books I should read. When I was almost a citizen, Chris had helped my education. Then I got sidetracked. At first he didn't recognize me, then,

"Mitch?"

"None other."

He came round the counter, gave me a huge hug. Of all the things I am, huggable I ain't. Where I grew up, you touch another man, you lose your arm. He said,

"I'm delighted to see you."

I believed him.

Told him about Aisling and my wedding plan. He said,

"I know exactly what you need."

He disappeared into the back. The radio was playing Midnight Oil and "Beds Are Burning." Catchy tune.

The *Evening Standard* was lying on a chair, early edition. Gant's photo on the front page. I edged the paper round, scanned the story. It was being treated as a drug-related deal.

Chris came back, said,

"This is an Irish wedding ring, known as a heart-in-hand, or Claddagh ring."

I liked it. Caught a glimpse of the price and went,

"Uh-uh."

Chris said,

"Don't worry about that,"

and gave me a 50 percent reduction.

Time to go, he said,

"Hang on a mo, I have a book for you."

Produced a slim volume. I read the title.

Izzy Baia
by
Kevin Whelan

I asked,

"Any good?"

"Magnificent."

We shook hands, and Chris said, "Listen, come over for a meal some evening. Sandra would love to see you."

I assured him I would. We both smiled at the blatant un-truth. Some friends, they don't judge you on the lies you tell.

As I headed out of the city, the ring snug in my pocket, I had a song in my head, Trisha Yearwood with "Hearts in Armor."

It made me sad, but not in any way that worried me.

N EXT UP, I went to Regent Street. I'd promised myself if I ever got flush, I'd buy shoes. Not any shoes, but Weejun. The assistant was better dressed than my bank manager. Same sneer, though. He said,

"How may I help you, sir?"

"You could talk right for a start."

Where do they learn that shit? Is there a school where they grind them in sarcasm and arrogance? I said,

"Pair of Weejun, size ten, tan . . . got it?"

He did.

Put them on and went to shoe heaven.

"Does sir find them satisfactory?"

"Beaut. I'll have two more pairs in black and brown."

The bill was gulp stuff. I gulped. Sneer asked,

"Cash or charge?"

I laid down a wedge, said,

"Take a wild guess."

Then he did the shoe con of

"Those shoes require careful cleaning."

He began to pile tubes on the counter, I said,

"Naw."

"Sir?"

"You can't beat a spit and a cloth."

"As sir wishes."

I took my packages, said,

"I'll miss you, pal."

He didn't reply.

You gonna shop, you have to take a pit stop. Do the mandatory designer coffee trip. I could do that.

The Seattle Coffee Company. They had coffee nine different ways to Sunday. I ordered a latte. Saying it, you have an instant lisp. The counter assistant was an in-your-face fake friendly. Her name tag read DEBI. She asked,

"Like a shot of something in that, sir?"

"Sure; nut a large Scotch in there."

She gave the tolerant smile, said,

"We have

     vanilla

         blackcurrant

             maple."

"Whoa, Debi, just the caffeine."

Plonked myself on the sofa and grabbed a paper. The latte tasted like foam and air. I read about "heshers"—thirteen-year-olds into heavy metal—and "tweakers"—fifteen-year-olds addicted to crystal meth, known as crank or speed. On weekends, they went out with the gang:

"Endlessly cruising the same shopping centers and ghost slot machine arcades."

Getting stoned

drunk

partying

fighting.

Anything to kill the boredom.

The only punctuation was

jail

abortion

suicide.

I put down the paper. The assistant came over, said,

"Would you like a loyalty card?"

"What?"

"Each time you come in, we punch your card, and then, after your tenth visit, you get a free coffee."

"I don't do loyalty."

"I beg your pardon?"

"No offense, Debi, but you're far too young to punch my card."

Outside a guy asked me if I wanted to score some dope. I looked round; no one seemed concerned he was plying his trade in blatant and broad daylight. I asked,

"Do you do loyalty cards?"

ARRIVING AT Aisling's, my heart was pounding. When she opened the door, I went,

"Wow!"

She was wearing one of those sheath dresses. Looked like a slip that shrank. My eyes fell to her cleavage. She said,

"The miracle of Wonderbra."

How could I not say,

"Wunderbar."

Inside, we kissed till she pushed me away, saying,

"Phew . . . I have dinner cooking."

"Me too."

She produced Jameson, said,

"Let us begin, Oirish; would you like a hot one?"

"I'm not even going to pretend I have the obvious reply."

I gave her the book Chris had given me, said,

"I had to search London to get you a Galway author."

She squealed,

"Kevin Whelan! I love him!"

I said, "And . . ."

Produced the box. She took it slowly, opened it carefully, went,

"Oh my God!"

It fit.

THE SMELL of good food cooking wafted from the kitchen. I had a look at a framed poem on the wall. It was by Jeff O'Connell. It read:

> SUFFERING SHIPWRECK
> *He sought the very moment*
> *when one emotion became its opposite,*
> *As if there he could find the explanation*
> *that might excuse his callous treatment of her.*

It gave me an eerie feeling. Like I'd just had my palm read. Aisling asked,

"What do you think?"

"Phew."

"Which means?"

I meant, or think I meant, someone walked on my grave. I asked,

"Where's he from?"

I heard her laugh, then say,

"That's so Irish."

"What?"

"Answer a question with a question."

"Oh."

"He's from Galway, the home of the Claddagh ring. Isn't that odd?"

I thought it was downright spooky.

KEEPING THE Irish theme, the Fureys were doing "Leaving Nancy," and we'd made hot international love. She asked,

"Do you love me?"

"I'm getting there."

"And will you marry me?"

"I'd say so."

"When?"

"Soon as."

She sat up,

"Oh my God, are you serious?"

"I am."

She ran from the bed and returned with the champagne, said,

"You know, we were to have Black Velvet."

"Yeah?"

In a perfect mimicry of me, she said,

"Screw the Guinness."

I was as near to happy as I'd ever get. That's pretty close.

I tried to do a bad brogue, asked,

"Will you be wanting the wedding to be big?"

"I'll be wanting it to be soon."

Love or its neighbor must have made me selfish or heedless or simply an asshole. I'm reaching . . . trying to lay off the fact that I didn't check on Briony. Not even a phone call.

TWO NIGHTS later, I was deep in sleep at Holland Park. It took the phone some ringing to pull me awake. Finally, I grabbed for the phone, muttered,

"What?"

"Mr. Mitchell?"

"Yeah."

"It's Dr. Patel."

"Who? . . . Oh yeah . . . Jeez, what time is it?"

"Two thirty . . . there's an emergency . . . it's Briony."

I sat up.

"Is she OK?"

"She's apparently taken an overdose."

"Apparently? What are you doing . . . guessing?"

"I'm trying my best, Mr. Mitchell."

"Yeah, yeah, I'm on my way."

I thought—"No better time to give my new BMW a run." I also thought that no way could it really be red. Not even Lillian Palmer could pull off a red BMW.

It was. Bright fucking red.

Well, leastways it was night. How much could it show? Glided up toward the lights in Notting Hill Gate. It was a dream drive. As I waited for the light to change, a blue Mazda cruised up beside me. Packed with brothers, rap streaming. My window was down, and the driver checked me out, said,

"Bro, dat be a righteous color." I nodded. He reached over, handed me a jay, said, "Rig like dat, yo gots to git down."

I took it, inhaled deep. The light went green, and the driver gunned his engine, said,

"Y'all be cool."

The dope kicked, and my vision blurred. I nearly did a cyclist at the Elephant and Castle roundabout. He shouted obscenities, and I answered,

"Be cool, bro."

When I got to St. Thomas's, I parked in their doctors' allotted area. A uniform came bundling out, crying,

"Oi!"

"Yes?"

"This is reserved for doctors."

"I'm a doctor."

"Eh?"

"How much are you smoking? Good Lord, man, look at your pallor, when did you have an ECG?"

"I . . ."

"And cut out those burgers, you won't last six months."

I strode past him. Though with the dope, it was more of a mellow sweep.

I met Patel outside the ICU. He didn't shake hands, accused, "You're stoned!"

"So?"

"Well, it seems inappropriate."

"Is Briony conscious?"

"No."

"So what does it matter a fuck, then?"

I didn't know the rage was there till I tapped into it. The old "kill the messenger syndrome." He said,

"We pumped her out, she'd ingested seventy-nine acetamin-ophen tablets."

"Counted them, did ya?"

Spittle from me landed on his white coat, my fists were balled. Two seconds and I'd be battering him. He began to back off, asked, "Would you like to see her?"

"Take a wild fuckin' guess."

I had to suit up for ICU:

gown

mask

booties.

I felt like an unneeded extra on *ER*.

Briony looked dead. Pale as the very color of despair. A respirator was aiding her breathing.

I held her hand, and a nurse got me a chair. The nurse said,

"You can talk to her."

"Can she hear me?"

"Perhaps."

"It would be a first."

"Excuse me?"

"She never heard me before."

S HE DIED after six. Never made it to the dawn. Later, Patel took me to his office, said,

"Feel free to smoke."

"Thanks."

"I am so very sorry."

"Whatever."

"I had . . . feelings for her . . . I . . ."

"Yo . . . Doc, I don't wanna hear it . . . OK?"

"Of course."

The paperwork done, the doc said,

"You'll want her in the family plot."

I gave a laugh steeped in malice, said,

"The family plot is a shoe box."

"Oh."

He hung his head. I reached in my pocket, took out a heavy wedge, dropped it on the table, said,

"Burn her. Isn't that what you Indians do? Then plonk her ashes on your mantelpiece, and you finally get to have her."

I was walking away when he asked,

"What about her little dog?"

"He lost his head, it's a family trait."

At reception a nurse called,

"Mr. Mitchell?"

"Yeah?"

"I am so sorry."

"Sure."

"Will you want her raincoat?"

"What?"

"She was wrapped in a coat . . . would you like to take it?"

I gave her a long look, said,

"She was about your build, you keep it."

I turned to go when she said,

"It's Gant."

"What?"

"The coat, it's a Gant, American label—a very expensive brand."

I couldn't get to grips with that, waved her away. Outside, I tried to light a cigarette. My hands were doing a fandango. I threw it away, headed for my car.

Blame the events of the previous days, jeez, the previous weeks, or the dope, the booze, or the shock of Briony's death, or I'm just a dumb motherfucker.

Whatever, I failed to ask two vital questions.

(1) Who found Briony?

(2) Who brought her to the hospital?

No, I was intent on small damage. To lash out at the nearest. The uniform came striding out. I focused on his shiny pants.

It mirrored the spit in his soul. The miracle of dry cleaning hadn't filtered down to him yet. He folded his arms, didn't speak. Fine, I thought. Fuck you, Jack.

I reached the BMW. Along the front fender, gouged in huge letters, was

JURKOFF

I spun round, shouted,

"Call yourself a security guard?"

"Why not? You call yourself a doctor."

Pure white rage coursed through me. What especially galled me was the gouger couldn't spell. I asked,

"And you'll have no idea who did it."

He gave me a toothy smile, said,

"Nope."

Then the anger evaporated. I couldn't be bothered. Got in the car, pulled outta there. I can still see his face, writ in dismay that I just let it go. Felt dismayed myself.

Rest of the day, I drifted like a ghost through pubs in southeast London. I was there

I drank

but never touched base.

Later, at Holland Park, I fell asleep in my clothes. Woke to find the actress giving me a blow job. She stopped, said,

"Don't worry, darling, we're nearly there."

Then, I thought she meant bringing me to climax. As with most everything else, I was hopelessly wrong.

Nᴇxᴛ ᴍᴏʀɴɪɴɢ, I shaved, showered and put on fresh clothes. Felt fresher if not better. Working through a double hit of nicotine and caffeine, the phone went. I said,

"Yeah?"

"Mitch."

"That you, Jeff?"

"Yeah, listen, mate, I'm gutted about Bri."

"Thanks."

"Listen, mate, I need to talk with you."

" 'Kay."

"Eight this evening, the Charlie Chaplin."

"I'll be there."

Put the phone down, thought—"Was there an edge there?"

Then I shrugged it away, not Jeff, no . . . he was my mate. Fuck, he and I went way back.

Outside the house, Jordan was doing the garden. I said,

"No end to your talents, eh."

He looked up, didn't answer. I walked over to the BMW. The gouge was gone. Jordan said,

"I couldn't allow it."

"You did the repairs yourself?"

"Yes."

"Fuck it, that's brill."

"As always, Mr. Mitchell, you overstate the obvious."

MY MARRIAGE plans required a birth certificate and balls. I'd got one, hoped I had the other. For the meet with Jeff, I put on the Gucci jacket, considered packing heat but decided against. I didn't take the BMW. In southeast London, it would be snapped in a mo. Hailed a cab and told the cabby,

"Charlie Chaplin at the Elephant."

He didn't say anything for a bit, then,

"You know why it's called that?"

"I've a feeling you're going to tell me."

" 'Cause Charlie was born up the road in Kennington."

I didn't answer lest I encouraged him. Then, undaunted, he asked,

"Know who else lives there?"

"No."

"Greta Scacchi!"

"Gee."

We got there, I paid him, said,

"You ought to be on *Mastermind*."

"Want me to wait?"

"I'll pass."

He handed me a card, said,

"Gimme a bell anytime."

I'd torn it in ribbons before I got to the pub.

Jeff was sitting at the bar, a pint of Guinness in his hand.

I said, "Waiting long?"

"No."

"What's on your mind, Jeff?"

He took a long breath, said,

"That guy, Kerrkovian, he's disappeared."

"Good riddance."

"No argument there, but the kid has gone too."

"Kid?"

"The punk kid, the one you'd a hard-on for."

"So?"

"So, he was hanging with Kerrkovian."

I took a drink, rolled a cig, asked,

"Spit it out."

"Had you anything to do with it?"

"No."

He drained his pint, stood up, said,

"People liked that kid; word is you offed him."

"Bullshit."

"Thing is, Mitch, once you've buried your sister, you'd be advised to stay away from southeast London."

It took a moment to sink in, then I said,

"You're threatening me?"

"I'm delivering a message."

Seemed to me I'd been taking shit from people all day. I said, "Here's a message back."

I swung fast, caught him under the chin. He crashed back against the bar. I turned on my heel, walked straight out.

Not a sign of a cab. I half considered trying to fit the scattered card back together.

NEXT MORNING, my right hand hurt like a bastard. The knuckles were bruised and swollen. I bathed it and then poured antiseptic over it.

Stung?

Oh fuck. I dropped the bottle, let my head back and howled like a son of a bitch.

Put on my suit and checked my reflection. Looked like a minor league mob guy. Bottom feeder and not connected.

Went down to the kitchen, smelt good aromas. Jordan was at the stove, asked,

"Hungry?"

"Like a wolf."

I pulled up a chair, and he poured me a scalding hot coffee. The aroma was so wonderful. I was afraid to taste it. How could it measure up? He put a plate before me. It was eggs over easy, with crispy bacon interwoven. Got a wedge of that with heavily buttered toast, bit down. Ah man, like a childhood you never had. Jordan sat down, dug into his. He ate like a demon, as if he'd a fire that couldn't be fed. He finished fast. I said,

"Jeez, you needed that."

He gave a cold nod. I added,

"You're not a morning type, right?"

"I have a busy schedule."

Stood up, went to a drawer, took out a thick envelope, said,

"You haven't been collecting your wages."

"What?"

"You are still on the payroll."

Then he looked at me, slow, asked,

"Unless you are considering resignation?"

It crossed my mind to tell him I was outta there, in jig time. I said,

" 'Course not."

As he cleared the plates, he said,

"Madam and I will be out all day next Friday. Can I rely on you to care for the house?"

"That's what you guys pay me for. What is it, a hot date?"

"Madam is being interviewed by *Hello!* in preparation for her return."

"It's supposed to be unlucky."

"I don't believe in luck."

" 'Course not . . . do you believe in anything?"

He was surprised, said,

"Madam, I believe only in Madam."

As before, he was telling me exactly how it was. As usual, I wasn't listening properly.

I DROVE to Kensington High Street. Despite the BMW's color, I loved that motor. Went and got the registry office squared away. In ten days we'd be married.

To celebrate, I went into Waterstone's and bought Derek Raymond's *The Devil's Home on Leave*.

It fit.

Then to a coffee shop and ordered a large cappuccino, no sprinkle. Got a comfortable seat next to the window and settled in to read.

I put the book down, sipped at the coffee, thought of Briony. As a little girl, she used to say,

"Won't you mind me, Mitch?"

I'd promise with all the empty power and earnestness of a seven-year-old boy.

Got up quickly and left, drove to Aisling.

Derek Raymond said when you dream of rain it's a sign of death. It was raining now. Briony, at twelve years old, crying,

"I'd stand in the snow, with no clothes on, to look at you."

Phew.

Only later did I realize I'd left Derek Raymond in the window on High Street Kensington. Maybe he would have liked that, listening to the rain, the rich aroma of fresh brew all round.

I SPENT the afternoon in bed with Aisling. Later, I asked,

"Was it good?"

"Ish."

"What?"

"Just kidding, it was magic. I just want to lie here, feeling like the cat who got the cream."

The rain lashed down on the roof. I said,

"Good thing we're in."

"Better that we're in each other."

Argue that.

Aisling held her left hand up to the light, said,

"See my ring, how the light bounces off it?"

"Yeah?"

"Notice the very top of the heart?"

I looked. Seemed like a small golden heart. So? I said,

"So?"

"It's chipped."

I sat up.

"You're kidding. I'll have Chris's ass."

"No . . . no, I love it like that. It's perfect that it has a tiny blemish."

"What?"

"The flaw makes it ideal."

I didn't get this, said,

"Is this an Irish thing?"

She laughed out loud, said,

"It's a girl thing."

"Right!"

I took her in my arms, could feel her heart beating against my chest. I was about to say—"I love you."

It was right there, my brain and tongue in sync to deliver the words I had never used, when she said,

"Will you do something for me?"

"I'll give it my best shot."

"Peter Gabriel has a song called 'I Grieve.' "

"And?"

"Will you listen to it with me?"

"Like . . . now?"

"Yes."

"OK . . . but . . . are you unhappy?"

"This is the best moment of my life."

"Phew! Let's give Pete a turn, then."

As we listened, she held my hand in both of hers, her face in rapt concentration. I've no beef with Peter Gabriel, in fact I love "Biko," but this just didn't fit. The sadness and pain of his voice and the lyrics made you reach for a lethal Scotch. Finally, it was done, and she turned her face to me, eagerness electric. I said,

"Now, that is an Irish thing."

GOT BACK to Holland Park late on Tuesday night. Watched *South Park* and wouldn't have balked at adopting Kenny.

The actress appeared at my door, asked,

"Can I visit?"

"I'm a little beat, Lillian."

"As in beating your meat?"

Closer than she could imagine. In her left hand was a bottle and two glasses. Held by the neck as they do in the movies.

Scratch that, as they do in *old* movies. She asked,

"Can a girl buy her fellah a drink?"

Jesus!

I said, "Maybe a nightcap."

She handed me the booze, said,

"It's Dom Pérignon."

"Whatever."

I popped the cork pretty good. As is mandatory, most of the champagne went on the floor. People seem to regard that as part of the deal. Some deal.

Lillian was wearing a silver ball gown. I'm not kidding—she told me. I asked,

"Why?"

"I thought a little ballroom dancing would be novel."

"And you hired a band?"

"An orchestra."

I looked at her face, said,

"I can only hope you're kidding."

Sly smile, then, "I don't do kidding."

"What, they're huddled in the hall?"

I indicated my room, added,

"Gonna be a tight squeeze for the guys."

"They're in the ballroom."

I didn't even ask where it was, but thought, "How fuckin' big *is* the house?"

I'd never explored it, and come Friday, when they were *Hello!*-ing, I'd go through it like a dervish. Yeah, shake them branches, see what shook free.

We clinked glasses and I said,

"*Sláinte.*"

She asked, "What is that?"

"Irish."

She shook herself in mock disgust, uttered,

"A nation of buffoons and blarney."

"Gee, how English of you."

She moved closer, said,

"Allow me to French you."

I did.

Her perfume was mothballs in chlorine. Blame the champagne, but I came. Not in a spectacular way due to my exertions with Aisling, more a sad drizzle. Like rain they get in Crete.

Wiping her mouth, she said,

"We need to get lead in that pencil."

I said, "You've exhausted me, there's no way I'll get to the dance."

She bought it, said,

"We'll dance tomorrow, now sleep, my sweet."

When she'd gone, I took a scalding shower, couldn't quite rid myself of her touch. In bed, I tried to think of Aisling, tried not to think of Briony.

Neither worked.

THE CALL CAME at two o'clock on Wednesday afternoon. I
picked up the phone, identified myself as "Yes" to
"Mr. Mitchell?"

It was the police.

"Are you familiar with one Aisling Dwyer?"

"Yes."

"I regret to inform you there's been a tragic accident."

"What?"

"A piece of paper in her purse listed your name and number."

"How is she,

    where,

        when,

            oh God."

I got the address of the Islington hospital and drove over.

I don't even remember the series of events. Only that she was
dead, from a hit-and-run on the High Street. A man had leant
over, held her hand until the ambulance came. Some time later,
someone gave me a coffee. It tasted like the foam cup. Then I
was given the "brown envelope." Her possessions.

It held

money

purse

calling card

watch

no ring.

Must have left it at home. I was surprised she'd taken it off.

At an early hour of Thursday morning, I drove home. Drank lights out.

I SURFACED around noon on Friday. Jesus, I was shook. My fingers fandangoed again as I tried to roll a smoke. Sweat cascaded down my forehead, stinging my eyes. I knew a shot of Scotch would shut the works down, but would I stop?

Would I fuck.

Went to my minifridge, got a brewski. Foster's.

When did I buy that, or worse . . . why?

Never-no-mind.

Popped the ring, drank full. It poured down my chin, drenching my sodden T-shirt. Then, à la Richard Dreyfuss in *Jaws*, I crushed the can, slung it.

Did its minijob, and my system eased. Took a shower, shaved, changed into a white shirt, fresh black jeans. Risked a mirror glance.

Like any seedy waiter.

OK, time to forage.

The house was silent, they really had gone. I avoided Lillian's room. It was already too familiar. Took a time till I located Jordan's. Knew it must be his as the door was locked. Braced myself against the far wall and took a flying kick. Near took it off the hinges.

I entered cautiously—booby traps were a definite possibility.

The room was Spartan, with an army-style cot, spit-made.

I went through the wardrobes first. Half a dozen black suits, black shoes and white shirts. On a top shelf was a shoe box that held a .454 Casull. It is one heavy mother. In every sense not too accurate, but the load it packs would blow a hole in an elephant. I put it gingerly in the waistband above my ass. Three drawers to go. First held spotlessly clean underwear. The second had a pile of old theater programs, all Lillian, of course. Finally, a storm of socks, put my hand through them. Pulled out a dog collar, said,

"What?"

It had dried blood and a name. Bartley-Jack.

Before I could react, my other hand touched a ring. Held it up to the light, the heart displaying the tiny flaw she so admired. I sank back on the bed, my mind reeling.

I THINK I must have made a subaudible noise. It's when people under total stress speak aloud without realizing it. Everybody does it, but some are more prone. I'd never be more prone than then. The sound is below normal hearing range. Years ago, it was called "thoughts in the throat." 'Course, the higher the stress, the louder the sound. Mine was heard, all right.

A voice said,

"Ah, the penny droppeth!"

Jordan was leaning against the shattered door, his arms folded. It took me a bit to find some voice, but eventually,

"You killed them all . . .

Briony

the dog

Aisling?"

He nodded.

"Christ Almighty . . . *all* of them?"

"Obstacles."

"What!"

"To Lillian."

"You're a fuckin' psycho."

"How trite, how utterly predictable."

I gut-shot him.

They say it's the most intense pain in the world. Slumped in the doorway, he wasn't arguing it. I stepped over him, and he grabbed at my ankle, said,

"Finish it."

"Get fucked—" and I kicked him in the balls. Double his bet.

LILLIAN WAS sitting up in bed, a pink shawl on her shoulders.

She gave me a smile, asked,

"What was that commotion, darling?"

"The butler did it."

I lazily raised the gun at her, and she asked in a petulant voice,

"Oh silly, really, how am I supposed to react?"

My turn to smile. I said,

"You're an actress. Try acting scared."